D0859435

the last
LOBO

the last
LOBO

ROLAND SMITH

hyperion books for children
new york

Printed in the United States of America.

First Edition
1 3 5 7 9 10 8 6 4 2

The text for this book is set in Centaur MT.

Library of Congress Cataloging-in-Publication Data
Smith, Roland, 1951–
The last lobo/by Roland Smith.
p. cm.
Summary: When Jake, a teenager, takes his grandfather
on a visit to their Hopi tribal homeland in Arizona,
he finds himself fighting to save an endangered Mexican wolf.
ISBN 0-7868-0428-9 (hc).—ISBN 0-7868-2378-X (library)
I. Hopi Indians—Juvenile Fiction. [1. Hopi Indians—Fiction. 2.
Grandfathers—Fiction. 3. Wolves—Fiction. 4. Indians of North
America—Arizona—Fiction. 5. Arizona—Fiction.] I. Title.
PZ7.S65766Las 1999 98-42656

For John Robert, with all my love . . .
Gramps

the last
LOBO

o n e

"What do you mean, Taw left?" I asked.

"He took off three weeks ago," Pete said. "He wouldn't even let me drive him to the airport. A cab came by and picked him up."

"Arizona?"

"Yep. He said he was going to Hopiland, but I haven't heard a word from him since he left. I called down there a couple of times, and the woman who answered the phone said she had seen him around, but the town he's living in doesn't have a phone or electricity. I left a message for him to call, but he hasn't yet."

"He was supposed to wait for me."

"I know, but he didn't know when you were coming back. Or if you were coming back."

"I don't believe this!" I looked around my grandfather's simple room. The mattress was stripped, the walls bare, the dresser drawers open and empty. Taw had been living at the retirement home for several years, and I thought he was content. "How could you let him leave?"

I regretted the accusation as soon as it left my mouth. Pete frowned. He had been a nurse at the home for years and was very close to my grandfather. If anyone could have talked Taw out of leaving, it would have been Pete. "He's a voluntary resident," he said slowly, "free to leave whenever he wants. I tried to get ahold of your father and you in Brazil, but I couldn't reach you."

"Sorry, Pete. I know you must have tried everything to keep him here. I'm just so shocked—and worried—to find him gone."

Pete's frown relaxed a bit. "That makes two of us."

"The jaguar preserve is pretty remote, and Doc doesn't have all the telecommunication equipment yet. He's got his funding now, but it will still take a while for the gear to arrive from the States and make it upriver to the preserve."

Pete walked over to the window and looked out. "I'm really sorry, Jake. I tried everything I could to stop him. I even thought about flying down to Arizona and seeing if I could talk him into coming back, but I couldn't get the time off."

Pete worked two jobs to support his family. When he finished at the home, he worked the late shift at the hospital.

"So what did he do with his stuff?" I asked.

Pete walked over and sat on the edge of the bed. "Some old people are collectors, surrounding themselves with everything they've ever owned. Others are simplifiers and get rid of everything they can't take with them when their time comes. Taw is in the second group. I helped him pack what he had in boxes and we stored them in the basement."

"Why did he pack his stuff away?"

"I don't think he's coming back, Jake."

"He's in no condition to live on his own."

"I agree, but unless your dad gets some kind of court order requiring mandatory supervision, Taw is free to do whatever he wants."

"Maybe I could get a court order."

"Not at fifteen, you can't. Your dad's the only one who can get the order, but he would have to be here to do it."

I sat down on the bed. It could take weeks to reach Doc in Brazil.

"How was Taw when he left?"

"To tell you the truth, he was the best I've ever seen him. His mind was clear. He hadn't had a slip since you left for Brazil."

Taw's brain occasionally drifted away. Sometimes these spells lasted a few minutes, sometimes several hours, and there was never any warning. Taw could be talking to you and disappear in midsentence. When he came back he wasn't aware that he had been gone. This wasn't a problem in the home under supervision, but when he was on his own, the spells could be disastrous.

"What did he take with him?"

"Just a little bag."

"Did he say anything about what he's going to do?"

"Just that he was going home. He left a package for you. It's in your room."

Before I went to Brazil to visit my father, I'd lived at the home for a few months while I went to school—a strange but interesting experience. I stood up. "I'll go check out the package. Maybe Taw left some clue about what he is thinking."

When I opened the door, a half dozen eavesdropping residents stumbled backward against the hallway wall.

"Jacob!" Mr. Clarke said. "I didn't know you were back." As always he had a strip of silver duct tape on the bridge of his nose to hold his glasses up. Not very stylish, but practical.

"Welcome home!" Mrs. Mapes said. She had forgotten to put her false teeth in again.

"Hello, everyone."

They began peppering me with questions and comments.

"Are you going down to get Taw?"

"Will you stay here with us or go back to be with your father in that horrible jungle?"

"I can't believe Taw left like he did. He hardly said good-bye."

"He gave me his spotting scope."

"I miss him."

"It's not the same here without Taw."

"Okay, okay." Pete walked out behind me. "Let's give Jake a little breathing room, folks. He just flew in from Brazil and needs to rest. There'll be plenty of time later for him to fill you in on his plans."

Reluctantly, they stepped aside. I quickly walked down the hall to my room and closed the door. Despite my concern for Taw, I started to laugh. I hadn't realized how much I had missed my old friends until I saw them gathered in the hallway. They were all wonderful in their quirky ways. How could Taw leave them? *Why* did he leave them?

The package was on the bed—an old shoe box wrapped in dinosaur birthday wrapping. Inside was a

Hopi kachina doll. I took it out and held it under the light. Kachina dolls come in hundreds of forms—eagle, snake dancer, warrior mouse. The dolls are carved out of cottonwood root and painted. The doll Taw left was a beautiful wolf kachina, and it looked relatively new. I wondered where he had gotten it. Certainly not in Poughkeepsie, New York. In the bottom of the box was a note written in Taw's almost undecipherable scrawl.

Jacob,

Sorry I couldn't wait for you to come back. An old friend needed my help. I'll be at Walpi on First Mesa if you want to visit.

All my love, Taw

I wondered who the old friend was. Taw rarely talked about his past. What little I knew of his days on the reservation came from my father.

My grandfather's Hopi name is Tawupu, which means Rabbit Skin Blanket. He was born in the village of Walpi on the very tip of First Mesa. When he was born his mother swaddled him in a rabbit skin blanket. Every time she took him out of the blanket he threw a tantrum, so on the twentieth day during the naming ceremony she chose to call him Tawupu.

My father, Robert Lansa, known as Doc because he has a Ph.D. in animal behavior and hates being called Bob, was born on the Hopi Indian Reservation. When Doc was a boy, Taw moved him and my grandmother to New York City to get a job working on skyscrapers. As far as I knew, Taw hadn't been back to Hopiland since the move.

A few years after Taw retired from balancing on steel I-beams sixty stories above the street, the rivets in his brain started to pop loose. Sometimes when his mind wandered away, his feet followed, which had caused a number of problems. We moved him to a retirement home in the country near Poughkeepsie where someone could keep a close eye on him.

I wasn't about to let Taw wander around the desert in Arizona. I had Doc's credit card, and I hadn't unpacked yet. I went downstairs and asked Pete to drive me to the airport.

t w o

By the time I reached Denver via Chicago, I was about ready to keel over with fatigue. Both flights had been full and I'd had to settle for middle seats, wedged between chatty people, which meant no sleep. One more short flight and I'd be in Flagstaff, Arizona. I wasn't sure how I was going to get to Hopiland from Flagstaff, but figured I could catch a bus or something. I hoped this last flight was less crowded so I could stretch out a little. My row had only two seats. I sat down hoping that none of the people shuffling down the narrow aisle had the seat next to me.

No such luck. An old man using a cane limped down the aisle and stopped at my row.

"You'll have to put your cane in the overhead," the flight attendant told him.

"Certainly." He put it in the overhead and looked at his ticket. "I think you're in my seat."

"Sorry." I had taken the window. I started to get up.

"Don't worry about it," he said. "I don't mind the aisle. I can stretch my bum leg out better."

He was a thin man with white hair and hawklike brown eyes. He looked to be in pretty good shape for his age except for the limp and his left hand, which was wrapped in a thick bandage. I guessed he was close to Taw's age. He sat down and pulled a plastic sandwich bag out of his shirt pocket.

"Carrot?" he said, offering me the bag.

"No, thanks." I had just spent my last dime on a Big Mac, french fries, and a large Coke, which had not set well at eight o'clock in the morning. I hoped there was a cash machine at the airport in Flagstaff. I would need some cash to get to Hopiland.

"My name's Buckley."

"Jacob Lansa."

"You live in Flagstaff?"

"No."

Buckley waited for me to tell him where I lived, but there was no simple answer to this, and I wasn't sure I had the energy to explain where I had been the last couple of years.

"You look Native American," he said.

"My father's Hopi."

"Wonderful people."

"I'm going down to see my grandfather on the reservation."

"Which mesa?"

"First."

"Where did you say you're from?"

Here we go, I thought. "A place in Brazil that doesn't have a name."

"Sounds like a place I'd like. Tell me more."

I gave him the short version, hoping I could get through two years in five minutes, then go to sleep. Mom died. Went to Kenya to find Doc, who was studying elephants. Found him. Moved with Doc to Poughkeepsie to be near Taw. Doc went to Brazil to help a friend of his set up a jaguar preserve. "I flew back from Brazil yesterday to take my grandfather to the reservation, but he left without me." I looked at my watch. Six minutes. Not bad.

"Your father's Robert Lansa the field biologist?"

"That's him."

"I know his work," Buckley said. "I was a biologist up in Washington State. I retired years ago, but I try to keep up on things. His work is brilliant."

I had heard this many times before, but I didn't expect to hear it from a complete stranger on a flight to Flagstaff. I asked Buckley where he was going.

"Got struck by wanderlust," he said. "I haven't been down to the Southwest in a long time. Might even go down to Mexico. I haven't decided exactly what I'm going to do yet."

"What happened to your hand?"

"A burn. No big deal. So, you're going back to Brazil to live?"

"That's the plan."

"What do you do about school down there?"

"Correspondence courses. And my dad and his girlfriend will help me with my studies. She has a Ph.D. in tropical ecology." I didn't mention the fact that Doc's first idea was to ship me off to boarding school. His girlfriend talked him out of it.

"I've always wanted to get down to Brazil and look around."

"It's beautiful when you get outside the towns and cities into the rain forest."

The airplane took off. I reached under the seat to get my water bottle, and the kachina doll fell out of my bag.

"Hopi?"

"My grandfather left it for me." I handed it to him.

"Wolf?"

"I think so."

"This is a fine piece of carving. Do you know who made it?"

"No."

He handed it back to me. "I've always wanted to go to Kenya. Did you get to see much of the country while you were there?"

"Quite a bit." I liked Buckley, but I was too tired to talk. "You should go there sometime." I leaned my head against the cool window and closed my eyes.

"We're here," Buckley said.

The plane was on the ground, and people were already inching their way down the aisle to the gate.

"Wow. I guess I missed the whole flight." And I could have used several more hours of sleep.

Buckley waited for everyone to get past us before standing up. He put out his hand. "It was good meeting you, Jacob. Good luck in your travels."

I shook his hand. "Sorry I was such poor company."

Buckley smiled and got his cane out from the overhead and limped down the aisle. I was the last person to leave the plane. When I got inside the terminal, I asked one of the security people if they had a cash machine.

"Down at baggage claim."

"And what about buses? I need to get over to the Hopi reservation."

"They can help you at ground transportation. That's across from baggage claim next to the rental car area."

I took my time getting down there, stopping at the restroom to wash my face and brush my teeth, which I hadn't done since I left Brazil the day before. I called Pete and told him that I had arrived and that I'd call when I got to the reservation and found Taw. He said he was still trying to reach Doc.

I found the cash machine, put Doc's card into it, and punched in the security code. I thought a hundred dollars would be enough to get me to Hopiland, but instead of burping out five crisp twenties, I got a message on the screen: INSUFFICIENT FUNDS! CONTACT YOUR BANK. I must have tapped Doc's account out when I bought the ticket to Flagstaff. I would have punched in a lesser amount, but the machine didn't give my card back.

"I don't believe this!"

"Problem?"

I turned around. It was Buckley.

"Yeah, the machine just ate my card."

"Isn't someone meeting you here?"

"No, I was going to catch a bus to the Hopi reservation. My grandfather doesn't exactly know I'm coming."

"A surprise."

"Something like that."

"I have a rental car. I'd be happy to give you a ride."

"That's nice of you to offer, but I don't have any money to pay you. And I'm sure you didn't plan on going to Hopiland."

Buckley laughed. "I don't have any plans, and if I remember right, the reservation is only about three hours from here. I'll tell you what I'll do. You can earn your keep by telling me all about Kenya. If you do a good job, I might be persuaded to throw in a meal on the way."

I grinned. "It's a deal."

He pointed at my backpack. "Is that all you have?"

"I'm not planning on staying long."

During the drive, I told Buckley everything I could remember about Kenya—the animals I encountered, elephant poaching, the drought, finding Doc, getting caught by poachers. I told him about my Masai friend, Supeet, and how he taught me how to stalk animals and borrow food from cheetahs.

It was the first time I had related the story in one sitting. It was clear from Buckley's questions that he was a biologist. He quizzed me on every little detail. The three hours it took us to get to First Mesa went by so fast, we didn't even bother to stop and eat.

"This is it," Buckley said, taking the winding road from Polacca to the top of First Mesa.

I had been to Arizona twice before. Once was when I was a little kid with my parents. Doc was speaking at a wildlife conference in Phoenix and we spent a couple of days on the Hopi reservation after he finished. The second trip was when I was eleven. Doc sent me down for a desert survival course. Mom had thrown a fit, saying I was too young, but Doc finally persuaded her to let me go. If I hadn't gone through that course, I probably would have died in Kenya when I got lost looking for Doc.

Buckley parked the Ford Taurus outside the visitor center at Hano, the first of three villages built on top of the mesa. We got out of the car. Lining the single, narrow dusty street were two- and three-story houses covered in whitewashed adobe. Laid out on blankets in the shade of the adobe walls were beautifully carved kachina dolls, baskets, pottery, and silver jewelry. The Hopi artists sat on folding chairs and on the ground talking with each other as tourists picked up, poked, and fondled their wares.

"I'll go into the center and see if they know where Taw is," I said.

I walked up to the girl behind the desk and introduced myself. "My grandfather, Tawupu, is staying at Walpi."

"I know him," she said. "But I haven't seen him for a while. You're welcome to walk down to Walpi. If he's there, you'll have no trouble finding him. There are only five people living in the village."

"Five people?"

"Old roots," she said. "Walpi is a traditional village. No electricity, no water. They carry their water into the village from the well or collect it from ancient cisterns. Not many Hopi choose to live that way anymore."

I couldn't imagine Taw choosing to live that way, either. He was a city person all the way. I went back outside and found Buckley squatting down, talking to one of the kachina carvers about his work.

"These are fabulous carvings," he said. "The last time I was down here, the kachina carvings weren't nearly as good."

"The style has changed over the years," the man said. "And we have much better equipment."

"I'd like to learn more about how you carve."

"I spent my whole life learning how to carve. My father taught me, his father taught him, and so on."

I think Buckley was after more hands-on information. He stood up. "Did you find out where your grandfather is?" he asked me.

"He's living in Walpi, but the woman inside wasn't certain he's there. I sure appreciate you driving me over here."

"I enjoyed it, Jake."

"Well, I guess I'll walk down to Walpi and see what's going on."

"Can I tag along? I'd like to meet your grandfather."

"Sure."

We walked down the narrow street through Hano and the second village, Sichomovi. As we walked, the mesa narrowed. In some places it wasn't more than a hundred feet wide with steep drop-offs on either side. Taw was used to heights, but this was not a good place for him to be wandering around. If his mind slipped and his feet followed, he could get himself killed with one misstep.

Walpi was built on the tip of the long mesa and presented a beautiful view of the rust-colored desert below.

"If I remember my pueblo history right," Buckley said, "the original Walpi was built in the eleven hundreds at the foot of First Mesa. In the sixteen hundreds the Hopi and other pueblo people rebelled against the Spanish and booted them out. They rebuilt Walpi on top of the mesa so they could defend themselves more easily if the Spanish returned. Some of these homes here are hundreds of years old."

It was like a ghost town. The only sound was the wind blowing sand between the adobe dwellings. We walked into the plaza at the center of the village and found an old woman in a long black dress sitting near a kiva weaving a basket.

"My name's Jacob Lansa. I'm looking for my grandfather, Tawupu."

She looked up slowly from her work and squinted at me with her dark eyes for a long time. "You look like him," she said. "Like he used to look when he was young. Who's this?" She nodded toward Buckley.

Buckley introduced himself.

"You're not Hopi."

"No."

"Are you here for the wolf?"

"I'm afraid I don't know anything about that," Buckley said.

"What wolf?" I asked.

"I heard it last night," the old woman said. "Woke me up. It's killing animals, they say. But I think it's a Skinwalker. One of those Navajo mischief makers causing trouble for the Hopi and disturbing an old woman's dreams. When the lobo is killed, the hunters will find a man lying there, not a wolf. When Skinwalkers die, they turn back into their human form."

"I heard they were introducing Mexican gray wolves into the Southwest," Buckley said. "But I didn't think it was anywhere near here."

"I am a hundred and five years old," she continued.

She certainly looked like she could be that old. Her skin was the color and texture of the windblown mesas.

"Have you seen Tawupu today?" I asked.

The old woman shook her head. "He left with some people a few days ago. John Sahu was with him. I knew John when he was a boy, too. He and Tawupu were always in trouble."

"Do you know when they're coming back?"

"Who knows, with those wild boys."

I grinned. Taw wild? Hard for me to picture. "Does John Sahu live here in Walpi?" I asked her.

"No, he lives on a ranch down below. Tawupu is staying here, though. Over there in his mother's home." She pointed at one of the adobe houses. "It has been empty a long time."

"Maybe he left you a note," Buckley said.

"I doubt it. He didn't know when or if I was coming, but we can check. Thank you."

"Come by and talk again, Jacob Lansa."

"I will."

She put her head down and continued working on her basket.

The inside of Taw's boyhood home consisted of a single medium-sized room. The walls were covered with whitewashed adobe. The ceiling was held up by rough-hewn timbers, and the floor was made of flagstone. In the corner was a simple fireplace. In the opposite corner was a pile of what looked like brand new tools—circular saw, drills, hammers, level, crowbar, assorted screwdrivers. What was Taw doing with this stuff? The only furniture was two narrow beds and a warped table with three rickety chairs. On the table was a map and a piece of paper with Taw's familiar scrawl. The first note was crossed out, but I could still read it.

Jake,

I'm staying out at John Sahu's for a few days. Ask anyone and they can tell you where it is. Someone will drive you out here if you give them a few dollars.

Taw

Below it was a second note.

Jake,

I'm camping at Chaco Canyon. We plan to be back by Tuesday.

Taw

"Guess he was expecting you," Buckley said.

"Guess so."

Buckley looked at the map, then looked at his watch. "We could get to Chaco by early evening if we leave now."

"I couldn't ask you to do that. You've already done enough for me."

"To tell you the truth, I've always wanted to see Chaco Canyon. It has the most extensive Anasazi ruins in the Southwest."

"I could just wait here. Tomorrow's Tuesday."

"Or you could earn your gas by telling me about Brazil and this jaguar preserve your father set up."

three

Halfway to Chaco we stopped at a restaurant. On the way in, Buckley bought a newspaper. "I want to check the classifieds for RVs. If I stay down here long, it will be cheaper than paying for hotels and a rental car."

While he looked at the classified section, I read the local news. "Hey, here's something about the Mexican gray wolf reintroduction."

Reintroduced Lobos Kill Livestock

ALBUQUERQUE, N.M. – Ranchers are up in arms over recent livestock deaths. Mexican gray wolves reintroduced last spring have killed at least six cattle in the past three weeks near the Apache National Forest.

"These recent killings may have been caused by denning females," said Dr. Rand McKenzie, chief field biologist for the project, at a press conference yesterday. "When a female has a litter of pups, she has to stay near the den site to tend them. During this time the male wolf does most of the hunting and cannot range too far away, because he has to bring food back to the female and her pups."

This explanation was little comfort to local ranchers who have lost livestock to the predators.

"So, next year we'll have more lobos to worry about?" asked Dayton Baxter, a rancher who has lost two prize cattle. "Those pups are going to get big and hungry. This is exactly why we got rid of the lobo in the first place. Wolves kill livestock. Plain and simple."

McKenzie expressed regret over the loss of livestock, but said a deprivation fund has been established, and the ranchers have all been paid fair market value for their dead cattle.

"It's not the money," Baxter said. "We don't want to drive up and see our animals ripped to pieces and strewn all over our private property. If I see a lobo on my land, I'm going to blow it away, and I don't care if they haul me to jail or not. I've had enough of this."

The Mexican wolf, or lobo (Spanish for wolf), was thought to have become extinct in the Southwest at least 30 years ago. The lobo is protected under the Endangered Species Act. Successful prosecution for the killing of an endangered species can include a prison term and severe financial penalties.

McKenzie pleaded with ranchers not to overreact to the recent killings. "If you find a carcass, leave it where it lies and contact us. When you remove the carcass, the wolves are forced to make another kill. By removing the dead animals, you are jeopardizing your own and your neighbors' livestock."

"I'll leave it lie," Baxter claimed. "And when the lobo comes back for seconds, I'll feed it a bullet for dessert."

The rancher was not alone in his sentiments.

Rand McKenzie was a friend of Doc's. He's Australian. Before I was born, he and Doc had spent quite a bit of time together on a field project in the outback. When the project was over, Rand came over to the United States with his wife and daughter, Nicole. They had been over to our apartment in Manhattan dozens of times. When he was in town, he helped Doc with the wolves at the zoo. I gave the article to Buckley to read. When he finished I asked him where the Apache National Forest was.

"A long way from Hopiland." Buckley spread the map out. "A good two hundred and fifty miles."

"Then the howl that woman heard didn't come from a lobo."

"Not likely. Probably a coyote. Here's our food."

Buckley had ordered a huge salad. I had ordered a burger and fries.

"Are you a vegetarian?"

"No. I'm just trying to set a good example. You

need to eat more fruits and vegetables, Jacob."

"How about a piece of apple pie for dessert?"

"That's not exactly what I meant by fruit, but you can have one if you continue the Brazilian adventure."

I concluded my story just after we turned onto the dirt road leading to Chaco Canyon. Plumes of dust billowed out behind us, and Buckley had a difficult time keeping the Taurus on the washboard road with his bandaged hand.

We reached the visitor center just as the sun was setting, and followed the signs to the camping area. It was jammed with RVs and tents. Buckley parked the Taurus and we started looking for Taw. It didn't take us long to find him. He was sitting on a folding chair next to a camper. Sitting next to him was an old man and a middle-aged woman. The woman was carving a piece of wood. A younger woman who looked about twenty-five was cooking something over the fire, and a little girl about four years old was helping her. They didn't notice us walk up, and I stood for a moment taking it all in. Taw looked wonderful and very comfortable camping, something he had never done before as far as I knew. His gray hair was braided in pigtails, and he had a red bandanna tied around his forehead. He was tanned the color of strong tea. He and the others were talking quietly in what I assumed was Hopi.

"Hi, Taw."

He looked up and shielded his eyes from the red sun dipping below the canyon. "Jake!" He jumped up and bounded over to me with more energy than I'd ever seen him display and gave me a big hug. "I knew you'd come!"

"What choice did I have?"

He held me at arm's length, ignoring my remark. "You look good. Come on over and I'll introduce you."

"I have someone with me," I said. "This is Buckley. . . ." I couldn't remember his last name.

"Johnson," he said. "Buckley Johnson."

I explained how Buckley had helped me to get to Walpi and Chaco.

Taw shook his hand. "I can't thank you enough. I should have anticipated the money problem. My son Robert gets his brain so filled by wild animals, he sometimes forgets about personal finances and other necessities."

That was an understatement.

"Come on over—we're just about ready to eat.

Everybody, this is my grandson Jacob and his savior, Buckley." He pointed at the two people in the chairs. "These two old roots are John and Betty Sahu. Your grandmother, Mary, was John's sister. That stunning woman cooking our meal is cousin Marie Yava, John and Betty's daughter. That would make her your first cousin once removed. And the little beauty hiding behind her mother is Hannah Yava. Hannah, this is your cousin Jake."

"Hi, cousin," Hannah said.

"Hi."

John Sahu appeared to be Taw's age, but his wife, Betty, was quite a bit younger, which explained how cousin Marie appeared to be only ten years older than I was. And she was stunning. Her black hair nearly reached her waist and was as shiny as crow feathers. She was slim and about my height. She wore jeans, running shoes, and a red tank top. She smiled with perfect teeth and said, "Welcome, cousin."

"I thought Jake was my cousin," Hannah said.

"He's my cousin, too," Marie explained. "Now, give him a squeeze."

Hannah was a duplicate of her mother, only three feet shorter. She walked over and threw her arms around my legs. "He's cute."

I picked her up. "You're not bad yourself."

John Sahu got up from the chair very slowly. Betty tried to help him, but he brushed her hand away irritably. He walked over to me, dragging his left leg. "Good to meet you," he said with a slight slur. "You look a lot like Tawupu when he was your age."

"An old woman said that same thing."

"Did she tell you she's a hundred and five?" Taw asked.

"Yes," I replied "And she said you and John were always getting in trouble."

John gave a lopsided grin. "That's Donna Pela, the oldest old root." There was something wrong with his left side. His left eye was milky colored, and his eyelid drooped. His left arm hung stiffly from his shoulder as if it didn't work.

"I think we should eat," Taw said.

Betty stood up and brushed the wood shavings from her long black skirt.

"Are you carving a kachina?" Buckley asked.

"I am," Betty said. "Are you interested in kachinas?"

"I'm more interested in how they're made."

"Do you carve?"

"I'd call what I do whittling."

Betty laughed. "There's little difference between

29

carving and whittling. After dinner I can show you how we go about it if you want."

"That would be wonderful," Buckley said. "But I don't want to impose on you folks. Maybe I should find a hotel."

"The hotels in Chaco have been closed for thousands of years," Taw said. "I think you should stay with us. We have plenty of blankets and sleeping bags."

"And food," Marie added.

"Well, that's awfully nice, and the food does smell good."

We ate a meal of lamb stew, roasted corn, and piki bread. Piki is made from blue cornmeal fried on a hot stone. The thin wafer is rolled and dried. It tastes like cornflakes without the milk.

"I didn't realize how much I missed this food," Taw said, savoring each mouthful.

He seemed to have shed ten years or more since I saw him last. I had a speech all prepared to try to persuade him to come back with me, but after watching him for the past hour, I wasn't sure I was going to deliver it. Maybe all he needed was to get out into the desert air and eat Hopi food.

"How was my neighbor Donna Pela doing?" Taw asked.

"She seemed fine. Is she really a hundred and five?"

Taw laughed. "I wouldn't doubt it. She was an old woman when we were young. She's outlived all of her children and most of her grandchildren."

Buckley took another scoop of lamb stew. The meat seemed to be agreeing with him this evening. "She told us that a wolf had woken her the night before. Or a Skinwalker."

"More likely a coyote," Uncle John said. "There haven't been lobos on Hopiland in a long time."

"I wouldn't be so sure, Dad," Marie said. "There have been a lot of sheep killed, and a few calves, in the last few weeks."

"Coyotes kill sheep and calves," Uncle John said. "So do dogs. It's not a lobo."

That seemed to put an end to the subject.

"One more course," Marie said, throwing a couple of handfuls of dried corn into an iron pot with a lid. She set the pot on the fire, and soon the corn started popping.

"Hopi popcorn," Taw said. "The best in the world." He stared off into the darkness. "During the war in the Pacific, I lay in my tent at night listening to small-arms fire in the distance. It sounded just like popcorn. At those moments I got so homesick, I

31

wanted to run across the ocean back to Hopiland."

I knew from Doc that Taw had fought during World War II, but I had never heard him talk about it. "What did you do during the war?"

"I was a Navajo Code Talker."

"What's that?"

"We were all over the Pacific. Orders and battle plans were given to us in English, and we relayed them over the radio in coded Navajo to another Navajo speaker who translated the messages back into English. The Japanese monitored our transmissions, but they never broke the code."

"But you're Hopi, not Navajo."

"My stepmother was Navajo. She made sure I knew the language. The marines thought I was Navajo. Because I was also fluent in English, I was an ideal Code Talker. World War II was quite an introduction to the outside world."

"When you got back, how long did you stay on the reservation before you moved to New York?" Marie asked.

"Several years," Taw said.

"You should never have gone to the House of Mica," Uncle John said.

"Looking back on it now, you might be right, John."

They might as well have been speaking in Hopi. "What are you talking about?" I asked.

John explained. "A thousand years ago it was prophesied to the Hopi that when a gourd of ashes was dropped on earth, we were to send a delegation to a place called the House of Mica to warn world leaders not to use this device again."

"When they dropped the atom bomb on Nagasaki and Hiroshima, the Hopi elders believed it was the gourd of ashes," Taw continued. "The Hopi elders decided that the United Nations building in New York was the House of Mica because most of the world's nations are represented there. My father was a member of the Hopi delegation. I went with him to New York."

"What happened?"

Taw laughed. "They barely let us in the front door. Too busy dividing up the earth to deal with the little delegation from Hopiland. I told my father that they wouldn't listen to us, but he paid no attention. He said it didn't matter if they listened or not. The important thing was to share the prophecy with them."

"And you stayed in New York?" I asked.

"No, I went back to Hopiland with my father and the others, but I knew I would return to New York."

Taw yawned.

I wanted to hear the rest of the story, but I knew I'd have to wait. One thing hadn't changed—Taw always fell asleep within minutes of swallowing the last bite of a meal. Without another word, he took his shoes off, put them next to the fire, then slipped into his sleeping bag, and fell asleep.

"Guess I'll go to sleep, too," Uncle John said. With some difficulty he stepped up into the camper.

"I'm going to stay up awhile longer," Betty said. "I promised our guest I'd teach him some things about Hopi whittling."

"I'm afraid I won't be doing much whittling until I get this bandage off my hand," Buckley said.

"You can learn a lot by watching." She lit a Coleman lantern, and Buckley followed her over to a picnic table at the edge of camp.

"Hannah, I think it's time for you to go to bed, too," Marie said.

"I'm not tired."

"You never are, but I want you to get into your sleeping bag, close your eyes, and see what happens."

"I want to sleep next to Cousin Jake."

"That's up to him."

"I don't mind," I said.

"Are you sure?"

"Sure."

"Okay," Marie said. "You go brush your teeth, little girl, and I'll move your bag next to Jake's."

I gave Marie a hand.

"Tawupu expected you every day," she said. "He left a note whenever he left Walpi."

"I got a little hung up in Brazil."

"I want to hear more about that. Taw hasn't stopped talking about your travels. We'll be able to find out if he was exaggerating."

"Well, don't hold it against him if he was."

"I won't." She gave me a couple of blankets, and I spread them out near the fire next to Hannah's bag.

"How's Taw doing?"

"What do you mean?"

"His health," I said, but I wanted to say, his mind.

"He seems to be doing just fine. Better than my father, I'm afraid. He had a stroke a year ago, and he's been very depressed. It's a miracle he agreed to come to Chaco with us. Since his stroke all he does is sit on the front porch, just wasting away. He's a little better now, but he still has a long ways to go. Tawupu has been trying different things to get him exercising, but Dad has stubbornly refused every suggestion except coming out here. I'm very grateful Tawupu came when he did, and resolved their feud."

"What feud?"

"It might be better if Tawupu explained it to you. It's ancient history."

I guess I didn't know Taw as well as I thought.

"What did Donna Pela say about the lobo?" she asked.

"Just that its howling woke her. Do you really think there's a wolf on Hopiland?"

"There's something there, and the ranchers are getting very upset about it."

Hannah returned wearing pajamas and crawled into her sleeping bag.

Marie tucked her in. "If I hear you bugging your cousin, I'm going to come out here and put you into the camper with me."

"I won't bug him."

"You better not." Marie kissed her good night, then joined her father in the camper.

"Good night, Cousin Jake."

"Good night."

"Tomorrow we'll go to Bonita."

"What's Bonita?"

"It's where the Ancient Ones lived. . . ."

"Hannah . . ." a voice from the camper warned.

Hannah closed her eyes. A moment later my little cousin was sound asleep.

I ate the last kernels of Hopi popcorn and listened to Buckley and Betty talking quietly about kachinas. The black sky was bright with stars. I fell asleep counting meteors and thinking about my grandfather.

four

I was walking down a street in Manhattan. Thick white clouds obscured the tops of the skyscrapers. I saw Taw walking ahead of me. I called to him, but he didn't hear me. I ran after him. As I got closer I saw that he was dressed for a day of steelwork in blue jeans, flannel shirt, and down vest. He wore a webbed safety belt around his waist and had a length of coiled rope over his left shoulder. In his right hand he carried his beat-up, black metal lunch pail and a stainless steel thermos. Following about thirty feet behind him was a large gray wolf.

"Watch out, Taw! There's a wolf behind you!"

He didn't hear me and disappeared into a fenced construction site with the wolf at his heels. In the center of the site was the steel skeleton of an unfinished skyscraper—floor after floor of girders and beams stretching upward through the low clouds. Taw was nowhere to be seen.

I heard a mechanical noise and followed the sound. It came from a construction elevator slowly making its way down to the bottom floor. I waited for it, hoping Taw would be inside. He wasn't. I opened the expanded metal door and stepped in. The door slammed shut behind me, and the elevator started back up.

There was nothing on the first three floors. On the fourth floor I saw my Masai friend, Supeet. He stood at the farthest end of the building on one leg wearing a red shuka, leaning on his spear.

"Supeet!"

"He needs your help," he said.

"Where is he?"

He smiled and pointed his spear at the upper floors. I hit the stop button several times, but the elevator continued up.

As I passed through the next two floors I saw nothing, but on the seventh floor I saw Doc standing on a narrow beam holding a radio tracking antenna above his head.

"Doc!" I shouted. "Dad!"

He was so intent on his tracking he didn't even look in my direction. I hit the stop button again, but it didn't work.

"Are you tracking the wolf?" I yelled as the elevator disappeared above him.

Doc looked up at me with a startled, haunted expression on his face, as if he didn't recognize me.

On the next floor I saw a black jaguar with a radio collar around its neck. It bounded nimbly from one I-beam to the next until it reached the end of the building, where it turned around and hissed.

"The cat's up here!" I yelled down to Doc. "You're on the wrong floor."

The elevator moved into clouds so thick I couldn't tell if there was anything on the floors I passed through. Finally, it stopped. I opened the door, but I was afraid to step out because I couldn't see through the clouds.

"Jacob?"

My mom's voice. "Mom?"

"Over here, honey."

I started to take a step, but stopped. "I can't. The clouds are too thick."

"The kachinas will protect you. Go ahead, honey. Just follow my voice."

I was desperate to go to her, but I was afraid I might fall if I tried.

"Please, Jacob."

I put my foot outside the door and felt solid ground. Tentatively, I stepped out. I felt around with the tip of my toe and realized I was standing on a narrow beam. I was just about to scoot back into the elevator when I heard the door slam shut and the screech of cables and pulleys as it started up without me.

"Mom?"

She didn't answer.

I called her over and over until I lost my voice. I sat down on the beam in despair and began to sob until I heard a strange clicking noise. The sound swirled around me and I couldn't tell what direction it was coming from, but it seemed to be getting closer. Suddenly, the clicking stopped and I felt something nudge me in the back. I turned my head around, hoping to see my mother, but it was the gray wolf. The clicking sound had been the wolf's nails striking the steel beam as it trotted toward me. I lurched forward to get away and slipped off the beam. As I fell, the wolf howled.

Someone grabbed me. He was dangling from his safety rope, holding onto me with his left hand. He was dressed like a kachina with a hideous mask on his head and Hopi blanket around his waist. His bare chest, arms, and legs were painted with black and white stripes.

The mask fell away and disappeared below us. The man holding me was Uncle John. "Where have you been?" he asked cheerfully. "We've been waiting for you."

"We?" I looked up and saw the gray wolf standing on the beam the safety rope was tied to. The lobo sniffed the rope, then started to gnaw on it.

I tried to yell. . . .

"Jake . . . Jake . . ."

I snapped my eyes open. Marie bent over me, gently shaking my shoulder. The sun was up. The bad dream was still pounding through my head.

"You were having a nightmare."

"More like a *day*mare." My head had cleared enough to notice that Marie was wearing running gear and was covered in a sheen of perspiration. "What time is it?"

"About nine o'clock."

I sat up and looked around. "Where is everyone?"

"Buckley drove them over to Pueblo Bonita. I came back to see if you wanted to join us. You sleep so soundly."

"I guess I was catching up."

"Do you run?"

When I'm being chased, I thought. I got up and rummaged through my pack. I found my running shoes and a pair of shorts, and we started to jog toward Bonita. Marie took it easy on me, but it wasn't long before I was gasping for breath. Marie was breathing as if she were standing still.

"We could walk awhile," she said.

"Why don't you just run ahead," I wheezed. "I'll catch up."

"Are you sure?"

I nodded, which at that moment was a lot easier than speaking. Marie ran ahead like a gazelle. I hobbled along, jogging until I couldn't breathe, walking until I recovered, embarrassed that she was in better shape than I was. About forty-five minutes after Marie left me in her dust, I arrived at Pueblo Bonita. I understood immediately why Buckley and the others wanted to go there. The ruin was huge, and several of the old walls were still standing. Marie was leaning against one of the walls waiting for me, totally recovered from her run. I was sweating like a racehorse. I took my T-shirt off and wiped my face with it. She handed me a water bottle. I emptied it and would have drunk a couple more bottles if she'd had them.

"This is Bonita," she said. "The Hopi believe they are the direct descendants of the Anasazi, which means 'the ancient ones.'"

It wasn't hard to imagine what it had looked like more than a thousand years ago when the Anasazi inhabited it.

"The others are over at one of the kivas," Marie said.

We found them standing above a deep circle cut in the ground with sides made out of sandstone blocks. The hole was more than ten feet deep and dozens of feet across.

"You're awake," Taw said.

"You're sweaty," Hannah added.

"This is one of the kivas John and I helped dig out back in 1937. What were we, sixteen at the time?" Taw said.

"You worked here?" I asked.

Uncle John and Taw nodded.

"What are the square holes in the bottom?"

"They're called the *sipapu*," Uncle John explained. "They symbolize the underground entrance the Anasazi used to reach this world. All the kivas here used to be covered by roofs, but they collapsed long before we came along."

"There's a kiva at Walpi," Taw added. "Not as big as this one. I'll show it to you when we get back."

"We use our kivas for ceremonies and meetings," Betty said. "They're built underground like this one. You enter them by climbing down a ladder through an opening in the center of the roof."

"How long did you work here?" I asked Taw.

"A year or so," he replied. "Our job was to dig out the walls and shore them up so they wouldn't collapse. Hard work. Hot in the summer, cold in the winter. Every shovelful of sand was supervised by the team of archeologists, which slowed things down considerably."

I leaned over the edge of the kiva to get a better look.

"Cousin Jake has a necklace," Hannah said.

Around my neck was a leather thong with the amulet Taw had given to Doc, and Doc had given to my mother. The amulet was made out of a round, flat stone about the size of a quarter. There was a hole in the middle and surrounding the hole was an intricately carved snake swallowing its tail. I had worn it ever since Mom died. Strung next to the amulet was a jaguar canine tooth I had been given in Brazil.

"May I see that?" Uncle John asked.

I didn't like taking it off, but I slipped the thong over my head and handed it to him. He stared at the amulet for a long time, then looked up at Taw with sad eyes. "Mary's?" he asked.

Taw nodded.

"I wondered what had happened to this." John took a deep breath and stared off into the distance as if he were remembering something.

We all looked at Taw for some kind of explanation.

"The amulet is Anasazi," he said. "From this site."

"They let you take artifacts from here?" Marie asked with surprise.

"No," Taw said. "We were supposed to tell them about anything we found so they could remove it themselves with their little trowels."

"So how did you end up with it?" I asked.

John and Taw looked at each other.

"I found the amulet right in this kiva," John said quietly. "When we got here, the kiva was filled nearly to the top with dirt. Each shovelful we hauled out was sifted by the archeologists with screen boxes. I found the amulet and pocketed it before it got to the screens. I gave it to Mary." He handed the amulet to Taw.

"And she gave it to me just before she died," Taw said. His eyes teared. He took a deep breath. "I wore it around my neck until the day I retired from the steel. After that I figured Jake's dad might need it more than I did. He wore it for a while, then gave it to Jake's mom."

And when she died I put it on and hadn't taken it off since. Taw gave it back to me and I slipped it over my head again. "Someone told me that it has power," I said.

John nodded. "My sister believed the power came from what the stone lay against."

I looked down at my chest.

"The heart gives the stone its power," John explained.

five

We stayed at Pueblo Bonita a couple of hours longer, then headed back to camp and got ready to leave. It turned out that Uncle John was interested in selling his camper because he could no longer drive it. Buckley was interested in buying it.

"You're going to get better, Dad," Marie said. "I think you should hang onto it."

"She's right about that," Buckley said. "I'm sure there are a lot of other campers down here for sale."

"*If* I get better," Uncle John said, "I'll buy another one. Why don't you drive my rig back to Walpi and see what you think? Marie can drive your rental."

"I don't know." It was clear Buckley didn't want to get in the middle of this.

"Oh, go ahead," Marie said, holding her hand out for the rental keys. "If he's going to sell it, he's going to sell it. Nothing I can do about it."

Buckley gave her the keys and climbed into the truck cab with Taw and Uncle John. It looked like I was riding with the women in the Taurus. Betty commandeered the passenger seat next to Marie, which left me with a spot in the backseat with Hannah. She couldn't have been happier, and proceeded to show me the toys stored in her backpack one by one.

Marie was not about to eat "camper dust" on the long road out of Chaco, so she made sure we left first, driving the Taurus as if we were competing in the Baja 500.

"Mom drives fast," Hannah remarked.

"I noticed."

I hadn't been able to get Taw alone to ask him why he had left the home so suddenly and about this mysterious feud between him and Uncle John. Every time I started to broach the subject, he wandered over to one of the others and started a conversation. I wanted to call Pete and give him an update, but I couldn't do that until I found out what Taw was thinking. There was no point in Doc coming all the way up here from Brazil if Taw was doing better at Hopiland than he had been doing at the home.

*　*　*

The road leading up to Hano was nearly blocked by parked cars and people. Marie looked over at Betty and raised her eyebrows.

"What's going on?" I asked.

"It's not a Hopi dance," Marie said. "I can tell you that."

She managed to squeeze the Taurus between a couple of old trucks and turned the engine off. She glanced into the backseat and saw that Hannah was asleep with her head in my lap. "She gets a little disoriented when she first wakes up. Can you carry her for a while, Jake?"

"Sure."

Betty asked one of the women walking up the road why everyone was here. The woman answered her in Hopi.

"The lobo," Betty explained. "It killed some more sheep, and they're meeting in Hano to discuss what to do about it."

It looked more like a party than a meeting. There were at least a hundred people milling around outside the visitor center. Marie started to elbow a path through the crowd, then came to an abrupt stop. She was staring at a metallic blue truck with oversized tires and a black roll bar with a row of spotlights along the top of it.

"Oh my God!" Marie said.

Three guys were sitting on the edge of the truck bed with their cowboy boots dangling over the side, smoking cigarettes. The one in the middle jumped down as soon as he saw Marie and gave her a big smile. "Hi, honey! I'm home."

His two friends laughed.

Marie was not at all amused. "Earl," she said flatly.

Earl was about six feet and had muscles bursting out of his T-shirt. His black hair was pulled back in a long pony tail and his thick arms were covered in tattoos.

"Did you miss me?" he asked with the same big smile, flicking his cigarette away.

"When did you get out?"

"Yesterday. Good behavior. You know how good I can be." He looked past Marie to where I was standing with Hannah in my arms. He stopped smiling. "Is that my daughter?"

He took a step forward.

"No, you don't!" Marie stepped in front of him.

"Put my daughter down!" he shouted.

Hannah woke up and started to cry. Betty took her from me. I walked forward to where Marie was standing. The two guys on the truck jumped down and took a couple of steps toward us.

50

"You better stay out of this, Jake," Marie said.

I stayed right where I was.

"Who's this?"

"My cousin, Jacob Lansa. He has nothing to do with this."

"He does now." He leaned forward and whispered, "If you touch my daughter again, it will be the last thing you ever do."

"We're divorced, Earl!" Marie shouted. "I have complete custody of Hannah. You have no right to go near her or me."

Earl looked around innocently. "Hey, girl, it's my reservation, too, and that divorce decree is just a piece of paper. We'll see if a piece of paper, or *you*, can keep me away from my own flesh and blood. I kind of doubt it. Don't you?" He stepped away from us and turned the smile back on. "Hannah, I'm your daddy." He started toward Betty. I took ahold of his arm. "Get your . . ."

"Jake Lansa!" A tall redheaded man dressed in jeans and a khaki shirt stepped out of the crowd. It was Rand McKenzie. "I've been waiting for you to show." He must have watched the whole scene in the plaza unfold. And he had stepped forward at the exact right moment. He turned to Earl. "Sorry, mate. I've got to get these folks inside before the meeting commences. You understand."

Earl did not look like he understood, but there wasn't much he could do about it. He leaned in toward Marie and said, "This isn't over." Then he smiled at Hannah. "Daddy will come pick you up and take you to Disneyland, honey." Hannah had stopped crying, but she didn't look like she wanted to see Mickey with Daddy.

"Let's go." Rand herded us into the visitor center and closed the door behind us. "Always in trouble," he said. "Just like your old man. Speaking of which, is he about?"

"He's in Brazil."

"Oh yeah, I heard about that. I saw you standing out there and thought I knew you, but I couldn't place the face until she said your name. Nearly blew me away. You've put on some bulk since I saw you last. What brings you to Hopi country?"

"I'm visiting my grandfather."

"Let's see . . . Tawupu, is that right? Where's he?"

"He'll be here soon. What brings you . . ."

"In a second." He looked at Marie, who was still shaken by what had happened in the plaza. She was holding Hannah now. "Who were those nasty bush-rangers out there?"

"The muscle man is my ex-husband," she said. "I don't know who the other two are. Probably cellmates. I appreciate you stepping forward, Mr. . . ."

"Rand McKenzie," he said. "An old mate of the Lansa clan."

"He talks funny," Hannah said, giggling.

"He's from Australia," I said.

"And who's this tacker?" Rand asked.

"I'm not a tacker. My name's Hannah."

Rand laughed. "*Tacker* means 'little person' in my language."

"I'm not a little person, either."

Marie turned to me. "Jake, I want you to stay away from Earl."

"Was that my daddy?" Hannah asked.

"We'll talk about that later." Marie handed her to Betty, who took her to the other side of the room.

"I'm serious, Jake." She turned back toward me. "Earl is bad news. He killed somebody three years ago. He was serving a ten-year term for manslaughter. I can't believe they let him out early."

The door opened and a girl about my age walked in. "Ahhh," Rand said, striding over to her. "Nicole. I was about ready to go out and find you. Jake, do you remember Nicole?"

I remembered her, but not like this. She had definitely grown up—rather nicely, too. The only thing

53

about her that hadn't changed were her eyes. They were still as blue as the Great Barrier Reef. Nicole was Rand's daughter. We used to play together when we were kids. Those days were clearly over now.

"Hey, Jake!" She gave me a bright smile, and I was surprised at how pleased I was that she recognized me. "Didn't expect to see you here."

My mouth had gone as dry as dust. "I'm surprised to see you, too," I managed to say.

"And I thought this meeting was going to be boring," Rand said. "Let's say we all get together after this and eat some food. Catch up on old times." He looked at his watch, then glanced across the room to three old Hopi men. "I guess we're ready, Chief," he called to them.

One of the men nodded and walked over to the door and opened it. The people came pouring in.

"How do you know it's not one of the lobos you let go over at Apache?" someone in back of us asked.

Rand had been standing up in front of the room fielding questions for half an hour. "Fair question. I know because yesterday morning before I flew out here, I located every one of our lobos. We have all of them radio-collared. They're not exactly hanging around where I would like, but they are nowhere near here."

The last time I'd seen Rand McKenzie, he and Doc were at the zoo moving the gray wolves to another enclosure. They crawled right into the dens with the wolves, pulled them out with noose poles, and put them into crates. The whole time they were catching the wolves, Rand was joking around as if they were handling a pack of teacup poodles. Amazing to watch.

"Then what do you think is killing our sheep and calves?" a man asked.

"Coyote, coydog, or dog. Has to be," Rand replied.

"Coydog?" another man asked.

"A cross between a dog and a coyote. There are a lot of them out here. I spent the day examining the carcasses and some of the places they had been taken. Two of the kills were clearly the work of coyotes. The other three I don't know about, but I can just about guarantee it wasn't a lobo."

"What are the chances of a wild lobo coming up from Mexico?" a woman asked.

"One in a million. There are probably fewer than a dozen lobos living down there. Some people think there are none left in Mexico."

One of the old roots sitting up front with Rand

stood up. "I'm sorry, but that's all the time we have. We appreciate you coming over here today, Dr. McKenzie."

"No problem." Rand took a seat in the front row next to Marie and Hannah.

"Is there anything else before we break?" the old root asked.

A man stood up in the back. "Just this. I've been authorized by the livestock association to post a thousand-dollar bounty on whatever is killing our animals. We don't care if it's a lobo or coydog. We just want the killing to stop."

Rand stood up again. "Hold on, mate. As I said, I don't think it's a lobo, but if by some miracle it is, you can't just kill it. The Mexican gray wolf is an endangered species, and it's protected by federal law."

"This is Hopiland!"

I recognized the voice. Earl. Everyone turned to look at him. I noticed that Taw, Uncle John, and Buckley had come in and were standing along the wall in back.

"We are our own nation," Earl continued. "And we can do what we want with the animals on our land." He flashed his smile at the livestock representative. "Your lobo problems are over, Mr. Higgins. You might as well make the check out to Earl Yava, because I'm going out looking for this killer starting right now."

About half the people in the room laughed. The other half looked over at Uncle John. He stared straight ahead without any expression whatsoever.

Earl and his two friends left the building.

s i x

After dinner we sat on Taw's roof in lawn chairs, enjoying the sunset. The view was incredible. We could see for at least fifty miles to the south, east, and west.

Buckley had decided to buy Uncle John's camper. He and Betty were driving to Flagstaff in the morning to return his rental car. Rand and Nicole were flying back to New Mexico later that night. He had flown over in the Fish and Wildlife Service airplane they used to track lobos. Taw and John had been unusually quiet since they'd returned from Chaco. Earl Yava had not been mentioned one time since the meeting ended, but I knew that he was on everyone's mind.

"I'll take you for a walk," Nicole said to Hannah.

"Okay."

"Don't leave Walpi," Marie said. "In fact, stay in sight of the roof."

"We will," Nicole said and climbed down the ladder leading to the ground with Hannah following.

"For the sake of argument, let's say there really was a lobo here," Buckley said to Rand.

"To tell you the truth, that could pose a dilemma for the reintroduction program."

"Why? I read that one of the problems with the Mexican wolf was that the gene pool was too small. That the lobos that are left are too closely related to one another. Wouldn't an unrelated lobo help the gene pool?"

"Yes, provided it was captured alive and in good enough shape to reproduce. In fact, it would be worth its weight in gold. But reintroducing a wolf into the wild has very little to do with biology, and as you probably know, everything to do with politics."

Buckley chuckled. "I haven't practiced biology in a long time, but I sure do remember that part of it. Can't say I miss that aspect. We had a word for it."

"What's that?"

"'Called it, *biolotics*."

"I love it, mate! Can I use that?"

"Be my guest."

"I'm not following you," I said.

Rand turned to me. "Sadly, reintroduction programs have more to do with people than they do

59

animals. You don't get anything accomplished for a species without first convincing people and politicians that it's the right thing to do. That's where the politics comes in."

"I guess I still don't understand."

"Well, let me relate it to our current situation," Rand said. "If there was a real lobo on Hopiland, it would very likely ruin the reintroduction program over at Apache National Forest. We ran into this problem in Idaho. We started translocating gray wolves, and then gray wolves started migrating across the border from Canada naturally. The opposition went to court, claiming that our reintroduction was interfering with the natural migration of the gray wolf, and they nearly shut us down.

"If the lobo started coming up from Mexico, the same case could be made. And this would be a good argument, if enough lobos were crossing the border to establish themselves here. Something like that could be enough for the politicians or the courts to shut the Mexican wolf program down. There are a lot of people out there just waiting for a reason to stop wolf reintroductions. We deal with these kind of people every day, and that's where the politics comes into it. The *biology* of a wolf reintroduction is simple compared with the politics. Essentially, you find a good spot for the wolves with plenty of food for them to eat and not too many people or livestock around for them to disturb, and you let them go. The biology part of it is up to the wolves, and nature."

"Are you saying that you wouldn't want to know if there were a lobo here?" Taw asked.

Rand laughed. "I would definitely want to know! At this point those unrepresented genes would be a lot more important than the current Mexican wolf reintroduction program. I'd be willing to trade the success of this release for some new lobo genes. But it's not going to happen, Taw. You don't have a Mexican wolf up here."

I looked over the edge of the roof and saw Nicole and Hannah talking to Donna Pela.

"So, what are you doing when you're not talking to people and letting lobos go?" I heard Buckley ask Rand.

"We're heading back to Australia. We've been pretty busy getting ready for that."

"How long will you be over there?"

"We're going home for good. Bought a sailboat last year. We have it moored in San Francisco, and we're sailing it across in six weeks."

"What will you do in Australia?"

"We have a good-sized piece of ground in the outback, and we're going to set up a research station there. It's been our dream from the very beginning. We originally came over here to raise money and make contacts for the station, then I got involved in wolf reintroduction and took a ten-year detour. It's time to go home."

Rand looked at his watch. "Speaking of home, we should be pushing off soon. But before we go, I wanted to ask you, Marie, about this Earl bloke. What are you going to do about him?"

"I wish I knew," she said. "I thought I had a few years to figure that all out."

"Do you think he was serious about taking Hannah?"

"I wouldn't put it past him to try," she said. "He was pretty upset when I divorced him. He wrote a bunch of threatening letters to me from prison. I wasn't too worried about them because he was locked up. But now that he's out . . . Earl usually follows through with his threats. That's about the only reliable thing about him."

"Well, I don't like the sound of that. Can you go to court and get a restraining order against him? Keep him away from you?"

"Sure," Marie said. "But that's 'just a piece of paper,' as Earl would say. It would keep him away legally, but not in fact."

"Where are you living now?"

"With us," Betty said. "But with John's condition . . ." She glanced at John. "Our place is pretty isolated. The nearest neighbor is ten miles away. We don't even have a phone."

Rand shook his head. "I don't like it. Is there someplace else you can go? A friend's house?"

"Earl knows all my friends."

"Well, here's an offer for you, then," Rand said. "I know you don't know me from Adam, but we would be happy to have you come stay with us. We have a big house near the national forest, and Sandra—that's my wife—would love to have a tacker like Hannah running around for a while. And if you like it there, we could perhaps work out an arrangement for you and Hannah to stay after we leave."

Marie almost started crying, but caught herself. "That is incredibly kind of you, Rand. But I have other things to think about. For one thing, I have to work."

"Where do you work?"

"Part time at one of the Hopi art shops along the highway. Doesn't pay much, but . . ."

"We're looking for someone in the U.S. Fish and Wildlife Services office," Rand interrupted. "It's not a great position, but I bet it pays better than what you get in the shop. Government work, you know.

I'm not suggesting you have to do this, but it would allow you some breathing room so you can decide what you really want to do."

Betty was vigorously nodding her head up and down.

"We have room in the plane," he said.

"Well, certainly not tonight," Marie said. "But I will think about it. Could I give you a call in the next few days?"

"Of course." Rand gave her a card. "How about you, Jake. Are you going to come over and pay us a visit?"

I was hoping he would invite me. "Sure."

"Want to pop over tonight in the airplane?"

"Well . . ." I looked at Taw. "I just got here."

"And I have something I need Jake to do," Marie said.

"What's that?" I asked.

"You'll see."

Rand stood up. "Can someone give us a lift to the landing strip?"

"I'll drive you over," Buckley offered.

"Are you staying with us?" I asked him.

"No, I'll stay out at John and Betty's so we can get an early start to Flagstaff tomorrow." Buckley seemed to be fitting in pretty well with the group, considering he had been here only twenty-four hours. If I hadn't known any better, I would have guessed he had known them his whole life.

"One final note about the lobo," Rand said. "If by a miracle someone captures an animal that looks like a gray wolf, give me a call. We can run some DNA tests on it to determine if it's a real lobo. Stranger things have happened. If it turned out to be the real thing, it would certainly help the lobo in the long run."

Rand shook everyone's hand. When he got to Uncle John, he said, "I've been racking my brain about your name, mate. John Sahu sounds so familiar, but I can't remember where I've heard it before."

"It's a common Hopi name," Uncle John said.

By the time I got a load of coal into the fireplace and lit it to keep the night chill out, Taw was in bed sound asleep. So much for quizzing him about what was going on. It wasn't long before I was asleep, too, but it didn't last long. A howl woke me up. At first I thought I was having the wolf dream again, but the howl continued after I opened my eyes. I sat up and grabbed the flashlight next to the bed and turned it on. Taw's bed was empty. I shone the light around the small room. He was gone.

I hurriedly pulled some clothes on and ran outside. The air was cool, but the rocks and adobe still held heat from the previous day. I was terrified that Taw had taken a wrong step and plunged to his death on the rubble below Walpi.

"Taw?"

"Up here," Taw whispered.

I was relieved to hear his voice. He was on the roof. I climbed the ladder. "What are you doing up here? It's pitch dark out."

"Did you hear it?" Donna Pela asked from the shadows below.

"Yes, Donna," Taw said. "Wonderful, isn't it?"

"Only you would think so, Tawupu," she said with disgust. "You and that John Sahu. I'm going back to bed."

"Lobos," Taw said.

"You heard Rand, Taw."

"Listen."

A howl floated across the night air from a long distance. A moment later it was joined by a second howl much closer to First Mesa.

"They sound like wolves to me," Taw said.

"When's the last time you heard a wolf howl?"

"When I was a boy. But it's not something you forget. Look!" Taw pointed.

About five miles away two sets of headlights were converging on each other, scanning the desert with bright spotlights.

"They won't get the lobo that way," he said with some amusement.

Or the coyote, I thought. After the meeting, we had heard dozens of people talking about catching the lobo. They apparently had already set dozens of snares and leghold traps all over Hopiland. By the looks of the two trucks, a couple of bounty hunters thought they could blind the lobo with a spotlight and shoot it.

The trucks stopped about ten feet apart. We heard voices, but we were too far away to hear what they were saying.

"Earl might catch the lobos," Taw said. "If he does, he'll kill them for sure."

"First of all, I don't think there are any lobos on Hopiland. And if there were, I don't think Earl would stand much of a chance. They don't teach wolf trapping in prison."

The trucks backed away from each other and headed in opposite directions.

Taw stood. "Let's go back to sleep." He climbed down the ladder.

s e v e n

When I got up the next morning, I found Taw back on the roof.

"How long have you been up here?"

"Since sunrise. I haven't missed one since I got back."

And I hadn't seen a sunrise since I got here. I looked at my watch. It was nearly ten. A warm breeze blew through our hair as we took in the view.

"It's good to be home," he said.

"In the note you left me, you said you were coming down to help an old friend. Uncle John?"

Taw nodded. "I should have come back here a long time ago."

"Why did you wait so long?"

"Embarrassment."

"About what?"

"A number of things." He looked out to the west. "Do you see that mesa?"

I nodded. The flat-topped mesa was four or five miles away and at least five hundred feet above the desert floor.

"When I was your age, I was as fast and agile as a coatimundi. John and I used to wake up every morning at dawn and race each other to that mesa. I beat him every single time, but he never stopped trying to win. We would climb to the top and sit up there for hours. John loved that view." He looked at me.

"Maybe you and I should climb up there," I said.

Taw shook his head. "Not without John. It wouldn't be right for me to go up there without him."

"I don't think Uncle John could make it to the top with his leg."

"It wouldn't be the easiest climb for me, either. I wish I could help John. I don't remember him being so stubborn. He's banned me from his house."

"Why?"

"Since his stroke he's let his house go. I thought if I started fixing it up, he would start helping me, but instead he told me to take my tools and leave." That explained the pile of tools in the house.

"I know he'll get better if he works," Taw continued. "John was never one to sit around. Neither was I, which I rediscovered when I got back down here. I haven't felt this good in years."

"Marie said you and Uncle John had a feud."

"More like a war," Taw said. "But I think we've made peace." He looked back at the mesa. "John and I were great friends, but we were different people. He climbed the mesa for the view. I climbed the mesa hoping the winds up there would bring an answer to my problems."

"What problems?"

Taw laughed. "The problems of youth. The biggest problem was that I could not picture myself living as a Hopi man. My father was a staunch traditionalist and expected me to become one, too. For many years I tried, but I wasn't interested in making corn grow in dry, wind-beaten sand drifts. I had no heart for the lonely work of herding sheep from one scant patch of grass to the next. In other words, I couldn't see myself making a living in the desert waiting for the kachinas to bring rain."

As Taw spoke, I imagined him as a young boy sitting on the mesa wondering what lay beyond the reservation.

"As I told you at Chaco, I went to New York with my father. When we were there, I looked up a couple of Navajo friends I met during the war. They took me up on the steel, and high above the streets I felt the same breeze I experienced on the mesa.

I knew what I was going to do. I came back to Hopiland, took Mary and your father, and returned to New York.

"John and Mary were very close, and he always assumed that the three of us would grow old together on Hopiland, but I changed all that when I insisted she and I move to the city. Mary was terribly lonely there. She missed her family, the land, and the Hopi life. She died of cancer two years after we moved there."

"And Uncle John blamed you?"

"Yes. I must have written him a hundred letters, and he never answered one of them. He lived alone for years and eventually met Betty. A wonderful woman. I sent a letter to John a few weeks ago. He threw it away without opening it, which I guess he had done to every other letter I sent over the years. Betty found it in the burn pile and read it. She called me at the home and told me about John's stroke and said that he had just about given up. I came down here to see if there was anything I could do to help him. But I think I've helped myself more than I've helped him."

"So, you're not going back to Poughkeepsie?"

Taw shook his head.

"Have you had any problems?" I asked.

He smiled. "You mean with my mind drifting?"

"Yeah."

"How would *I* know?" Taw laughed. "Seriously, I have to take it easy, but I'm doing a lot better than I was at the home."

"Pete's been trying to get ahold of Dad."

"I figured he would. He was pretty upset when I left."

"I'll give Pete a call and tell him you're doing fine, but it might be too late to stop Dad from coming up here."

"It doesn't matter. In fact, I hope he does come up. I miss him." Taw looked back at the mesa. "You know what I think you should do?"

"What?"

"I think you should run to the mesa and climb it. Tell me what the winds are saying."

"Now?"

"I'd wait until it cools down." Taw put his arm around my shoulders. "I appreciate you coming down here to check up on me."

About two P.M. a bank of clouds moved in and the temperature dropped. I put on my running shoes and headed to Hano to use the phone at the visitor center to call Pete. He was very happy to hear that

Taw was doing okay and said he would try to get word to Doc.

When I came out of the center, I saw a group of people gathered around an old truck parked in the plaza. Several were carrying rifles. Earl and his two friends were among them. Earl glared at me, but then walked away. I was relieved.

I walked over to the truck. Lying in the bed was a half-eaten calf. Not a pretty sight. The calf's owner looked down at the carcass.

"Third one!" he said angrily. "I'm adding two hundred fifty dollars to the thousand-dollar reward."

A couple of people shouted their approval. Someone would eventually bring a canine in—probably dozens of them—before it was all over, but none of them would be wolves. If they kept at it, there wouldn't be a coyote or stray dog left on the reservation.

I started back through Hano to catch the path leading to the desert, but I didn't get very far. Earl and his two friends stepped out from behind one of the houses. I tried to walk around them, but Earl blocked my way.

"What do you want, Earl?"

"I want to continue the conversation we had yesterday."

"There's nothing more to talk about." I tried to

push past him, but he grabbed my arm and slammed me against the wall, then pinned me across the chest with his rifle. He leaned forward until his face was about an inch away from mine and said, "I meant what I said yesterday about staying away from my daughter. That goes for Marie as well. If I see you anywhere near her . . ."

"Earl!" a voice said behind him.

Earl was too close for me to see who it was. He turned his head. I saw my opening, and I was about to jerk away from him when he suddenly stepped away from me.

"Leave him alone."

It was Donna Pela. She said something else to him in Hopi. Earl responded in Hopi, then turned to me and said, "This isn't over."

He walked off with his two friends.

I went over to Donna. "Thanks. What did you say to him?"

"It's not important, Tawupu."

I didn't bother to correct her. She looked down at my legs. "Do me a favor," she said.

"Sure."

"Let John win today."

She walked away before I could respond.

eight

Before I started my run I glanced back up at Walpi. It looked like a stone fortress. During his runs when he was a boy, Taw must have felt like a prisoner fleeing.

It felt good to stretch my legs and inhale the sweet sage-scented air. After a half mile it was clear I wouldn't be able to run all the way to Taw's mesa, but I was determined to get as far as my legs and lungs would take me. I made it about a third of the way before I started walking. I picked out a cactus in the distance and vowed to start running again when I reached it.

About halfway there I heard a horse whinny behind me. I turned around and saw two horses heading in my direction, but they were too far away for me to see who was riding them. I hoped it wasn't Earl with one of his pals. Donna Pela was not going to come to my rescue out here. I picked up a good-sized rock. David and Goliath.

As the horses drew nearer I was relieved to see it was Marie. She was leading the second horse. She cantered up to me and smiled. "Prospecting?"

I let the rock drop to the ground. "Running."

"Looked more like a walk."

I wasn't sure I liked my cousin's sense of humor.

"Do you ride?" she asked.

I shook my head. No sense in lying. If I got into the saddle, she would know the truth immediately. I'd ridden elephants, but I'd never ridden a horse.

She reached into her saddle pack and pulled out a pair of familiar-looking jeans. Mine.

"You'll need to wear these, or the insides of your legs will turn to hamburger after a few miles."

I pulled the jeans over my shorts. Riding to the mesa would be a lot easier than jogging, or so I thought.

When I put my foot into the stirrup, my horse turned his head and regarded me with what looked like mild disgust. Doc used to say that animals knew more about us than we knew about them. I mounted him and he started to buck. Maybe Doc was right.

Marie grabbed the bridle near the bit. "Settle down, Hank," she cooed.

"What's your horse called?"

"Heather."

"Not exactly Hopi names."

"I was very young when I named them."

Hank decided to cut the amateur cowboy a little slack and stopped trying to eject me. Marie swung off Heather and adjusted my stirrups.

"He'll be all right now," she said, climbing back on. We started forward at a leisurely walk.

"You saw Taw?"

"He was on the roof watching you."

"Where did you get the horses?" I didn't think Marie had come out here with the horses to give me a lift to Taw's mesa. She must have had something else in mind.

"I've had them since I was little. I'm moving them to a friend's corral in Polacca so my folks don't have to take care of them while I'm gone."

"You're leaving?"

"I don't want to, but I don't know what else to do. We're taking the bus to New Mexico later tonight. I'm going to take Rand up on his offer."

"I'm glad." I thought about telling her about my encounter with Earl, but decided that it would just upset her. "Where's Hannah?"

"She went with Mom and Buckley to take the car back to Flagstaff. They're meeting me later in Polacca to take me to the bus station. I've been running around like crazy trying to get ready to leave."

"Can I give you a hand with something?"

"That's why I rode out here," she said. "Taw says you heard the lobo last night."

"I heard a *canine* howling. I don't think it was a lobo."

"I was wondering if you could do me a favor while I'm gone."

"Sure."

"I want you to help my father catch the lobo."

I pulled back on the reins. "What?"

"He's very depressed about this Earl business. He thinks the reason I'm leaving is because he can't do anything to protect me."

"What does that have to do with catching a lobo?"

"His doctor says he'll recover if he stays active. If he sits around like he's been doing, he won't last a year. Trying to catch the lobo would occupy his mind and get his body moving."

I liked Taw's idea of fixing up his house better. "What does Uncle John know about trapping wolves?"

Marie smiled. "My father knows everything about trapping wolves. If there *were* a lobo here, wouldn't you want to help it?"

"Of course. If I could."

"Will you ride out with me to talk to my father about it?"

"I guess so."

Marie kicked Heather in the flanks and she galloped away. Hank took off after her like an artillery shell. He wasn't about to be left alone in the desert with me on his back. After about a mile my rear felt like it had been numbed with a sledgehammer. I pulled back on the reins, swung off, and found I could barely stand. "I must be doing something wrong."

"Use your legs to absorb the shock," Marie said. "That's what the stirrups are for."

Now she tells me. "It might be easier on my tender rear if we had the horses walk instead of gallop."

"I suppose it would."

I got back on, and this time we walked the horses over the desert scrub land. Hank seemed to be adjusting to having me on his back. I think he knew I was in agony, and this calmed him. Every once in a while he would glance back at me, and I swear he was grinning. I asked Marie a couple of times how far Uncle John's place was, but all she would say was that we would get there a lot faster at a trot. I told her to forget it, I had all the time in the world.

We rode across several fenced pastures. Some

had herds of cattle, some had flocks of sheep. When we came to a gate, Marie leaned over, slipped the latch, and swung it open without stopping. She handled her horse like a Plains Indian, apparently forgetting that our ancestors were agriculturists, not buffalo hunters.

"There it is," she said finally.

About a half mile ahead was an adobe house with several wooden outbuildings sprinkled around it. We crossed another fenced sheep pasture. Lambs bounded out of our way like large white rabbits. As we got closer I saw that Taw wasn't exaggerating about the condition of the house. Several windows were broken and had been replaced with plywood and cardboard. Large chunks of adobe had disintegrated or fallen off, making the house look like it had been bombarded. There was a series of solar panels on the roof for power. Several of them were broken.

"I'll go in and get him," she said. "There's a water trough in back of that building. You can tie the horses there."

"Yes, ma'am." I tipped my invisible cowboy hat.

Marie swung out of her saddle as if she were getting out of an easy chair after a nap. I got out of my saddle as if I had been in traction for a month. The horses led *me* to the water trough. I tied them and walked stiffly back to the house. Uncle John and Marie were standing on the front porch. Lying at Uncle John's feet was a very old Australian cattle dog that didn't even bother lifting its head when I walked up.

"Jake said he would be happy to help you catch the lobo," Marie said abruptly.

"If there is a lobo," I added.

Uncle John focused on me with his good eye. "There's a lobo," he said quietly.

I was surprised to hear him say this. At Chaco he claimed it was a coyote. I reminded him of that.

"I changed my mind," he said simply.

"Well, if it's a lobo," I said, "there are two of them. Taw and I heard them last night. The howls came from different areas, but they sounded exactly the same."

Uncle John gazed silently out at his pasture.

"Rand sure doesn't think there's a lobo here," I added.

This didn't even warrant a glance from Uncle John's good eye. "He's wrong," he said.

"With Jake's help you could catch the lobo before Earl gets his hands on it," Marie said.

John looked at her. "And what does Jacob know about catching lobos?"

"Nothing!" I said before Marie could answer for me.

"You've caught wolves at the zoo," she said. "Rand was talking about it last night."

"I *watched* them catch wolves inside a cage. Big difference."

John looked back at the pasture. Marie glared at me. "You could teach him just like you taught Earl."

What was she talking about?

"Not enough time," Uncle John said.

"So, you're just going to let Earl kill the lobo?"

Uncle John looked as though a yellow jacket had stung him in the face.

"If he kills it," she continued, "it will be all your fault."

The yellow jacket got him again, but he recovered quickly. "Jake doesn't even believe it's a lobo," he said. "You can't catch something that you don't think is out there. And Earl won't be able to catch it, either."

"What makes you think that?"

"I taught Earl everything *he* knows about trapping, not everything *I* know about trapping," he said. "Second, lobos are like ghosts now. The few that are left have been forced to move and behave like spirits in order to survive. Earl's never come across an animal like that."

"You taught Earl how to trap?" I asked.

Uncle John nodded.

"And he's very good at it," Marie added.

"Have you actually seen this lobo?" I asked.

"No, but last night Buckley and I found some tracks and followed them for as far as my legs would carry me. And I examined the scats. I heard the howl, too. It's a lobo."

"And you've trapped wolves before?"

"In Mexico, Alaska, Canada, and Siberia. But that was a long time ago, before idiots like me helped to get rid of them."

I didn't know what to say. From what Taw was saying earlier, I had assumed that Uncle John had never left the reservation. I wished Marie had told me this before we got here.

"I'd like to help you, Uncle John. I didn't know . . ."

Uncle John cut me off with a shake of his head. "Buckley and I were talking about it last night. He said he thought it was a shame that we can't just leave animals alone. I agree with him."

"The problem is, Dad, that people are not going to leave this wolf alone. Someone is going kill this wolf. Will you at least think about teaming up with Jake to catch it?"

He didn't answer her.

Marie looked at her watch. "We've got to go." She kissed him on the cheek. "Please think about it, Dad. I'll get word to you when we arrive at Rand's."

As we rode back she filled me in a little on Uncle John's trapping history.

"It all happened before I came along," she said. "But Dad used to make his living trapping animals. He worked for the predator control division here in Arizona, then started contracting out to other states and countries. He gave it up when he married Mom. He didn't like to be away from her."

"How does Earl fit into all this?"

"Earl and I went to high school together, and when we became an item, he spent more time at our house than he did his own. Dad didn't want to teach him how to trap, but Earl can be pretty persuasive. He talked Dad into it."

"It's none of my business, but what happened between you and Earl?"

Marie took a deep breath. "We got married right out of high school, and things went fine for the first couple of years. He couldn't find work, which is not that unusual around here. He had a lot of time on his hands and started hanging out with some complete morons. A lot of nights he wouldn't even come home.

I thought when Hannah was born he would change. He didn't. If anything, he got worse. He started slapping me around. I moved back home. He'd come by and harass us. Dad finally got tired of this and had it out with him one evening in our front yard. Earl wasn't lifting weights back then, and Dad whipped him good. That was the worst evening of my life. The police came and hauled them both away and let them go the next day. But Earl did stop harassing us, and I filed for a legal separation."

"What about the guy he killed?"

"I was at a dance one afternoon with a friend. Earl showed up and started pushing him around. Some men stepped in and broke it up and kicked Earl out of the dance.

"No one knows exactly what happened next, but my friend was found the next day beaten to death. Earl didn't do it alone, but his friends said he instigated it. He got ten years, and I thought I was safe for a while. End of story."

But now that he was out, the story was far from over. We rode on in silence.

About halfway to Walpi, Hank came to an abrupt halt. He started dancing around like he had stepped into a pool of molten lava. I hung onto the saddle horn and looked at the ground, thinking there was a rattlesnake or something down there, but I didn't see anything. Then I noticed about twenty yards ahead of us a herd of sheep was jammed against a pasture gate. They were huddled together and baaing frantically.

Marie tried to get ahold of Hank's reins, but he kept dancing away from her. She jumped off Heather and slowly walked toward him. "Whoa, boy," she calmly said. Hank stopped dancing so she could get close enough to grab the reins, but his eyes were still bugging out of his head.

I swung off. The sheep were still bunched together at the gate. The ones in front were trying desperately to squeeze through the narrow spaces between the aluminum crossbars. Something strange was causing them to panic. We had been through the pasture earlier and they hadn't acted like this.

I walked over to the gate and climbed up on it to get a better view. About a hundred yards out I saw a blotch of white that looked like a sheep lying down. Sheep don't hang out by themselves, and they don't lie down when there is something in the pasture terrifying them.

Marie led the much calmer horses over to where I was.

"I think there's a dead sheep over there," I

whispered. Suddenly, the dead sheep was jerked behind a sage bush. I would have given anything for a spotting scope. I jumped down. There weren't many things that could make a dead sheep move like that. "We might have stumbled onto something here."

"What is it?"

"I'm not sure yet." I had to get close enough to see if the mover was a coyote, coydog, dog, or lobo. There was a slight breeze coming from the south so I was down wind from whatever killed that sheep. I checked the sun. It was pretty low on the horizon— about two hours of light left. This could pose a problem. All I had to do was get close enough to see what it was, but to do that I would need to stalk at least eighty yards. There were a couple of bushes and trees I could use to block my approach, but even with these it could easily take two hours.

I pulled my T-shirt off.

"What are you doing, Jake?"

"Shhh . . . you'll scare it away."

"But why are you taking . . ."

"I learned to stalk animals when I was in Kenya," I whispered. "This is how I do it." I spotted a yucca on the other side of the fence. I reached through and broke off a couple of branches, then proceeded to take off the rest of my clothes, including my running shoes and socks, so I'd be able to "feel" the ground with my bare feet rather than look at it.

"You do it naked?" Marie asked, shocked.

"Afraid so."

Marie turned around. "You'll cut your feet," she whispered.

"I hope not," I said. "I'll be moving very slowly. I need my feet bare so I can feel what I'm stepping on before it makes any noise. You'll see."

"Not with my back turned, I won't."

I smeared yucca juice all over my skin, then rolled on the ground, trying to keep the sheep dung away from my face. When I stood up, I must have looked like some kind of monster, because Hank tried to tear the reins out of Marie's hand, but she held on tight. He wasn't sorry to see the sand man head south.

The stalk was difficult right from the beginning. The first problem was that my muscles were stiff from riding. The key to a good stalk is to move extremely slowly, picking each footstep with great care. To do this I had to raise my knee waist high and pause before gently putting my foot back on the ground. This motion sent spasms of pain shooting through my legs. The second problem was the ground. It was like walking barefoot through a nail factory. It sometimes took me a full minute to find a clear spot without a cactus spine or sharp rock. At this rate I wouldn't reach the south end of the pasture until midnight. My only choice was to increase my pace and take the chance of spooking the animal that was dining on the sheep. If I was lucky, I'd be able to get to within fifty yards, then start my slow stalk again.

As I moved forward I tried to keep trees and bushes between me and my quarry. To do this I had to crab-walk and sometimes crawl, which was pretty unpleasant with prickly pear cactus growing everywhere. By the time I reached the point where I started my final stalk, I felt like a pincushion.

I moved forward one painful step after the other with my full attention on the sage bush shielding the animal. Despite the fading light, I made myself inch forward. I wasn't about to blow it after all the work it had taken to get there.

At thirty yards I could see the sage moving. At twenty yards I could hear the dry branches rattle. Suddenly, the branches stopped moving. I froze in midstep and held my breath. A large gray head popped up and stared directly at me with alert yellow eyes tinged red from the setting sun. This was not a ghost. It was a lobo. It knew something was there, but couldn't see it. I was the ghost. There was blood on its muzzle.

The lobo turned its head away from me and stared west. Its ears moved in different directions, listening to something I couldn't hear. With just my eyes, I looked in the direction the lobo was staring and saw headlights dancing across the desert. They were moving toward us. When I looked back, the lobo had lowered its head and was working on the carcass again.

There was a dirt road on the other side of the fence. In a minute the vehicle was going to pass right by us. Now isn't the time to be eating, I thought. The lobo was aware of this. Its head came back up with a woolly haunch clamped in its mouth. It looked toward the approaching headlights, then turned and ran across the pasture, jumping the east fence with the grace of a deer. A minute later a familiar truck came down the road spewing a cloud of dust behind it. When it passed me, the driver flicked a cigarette out the window. The driver was Earl. The cigarette landed an inch from where I was standing. He continued on without a glance in my direction. I put the cigarette out with my bare foot.

n i n e

It was dark by the time we got to Polacca. As soon as we rode up, the front door to Marie's friends' house flew open and Hannah ran out, followed by Betty.

"We were worried about you," Betty said. "I thought something had happened."

"Nothing happened, Mom," Marie swung off, and Hannah jumped into her arms.

"We went to Flagstaff," Hannah said. "But I didn't see any flags."

Buckley came out onto the porch. "Hey, Jake."

"Where were you?" Betty asked. "The bus leaves in less than an hour."

"We saw the lobo," Marie said. "Well, actually, I caught a running glimpse of it, but Jake had what I'd call a close encounter with it."

Buckley came off the porch and started throwing questions at me. Where did you see it? How close were you? How big was it?

But I was surprised to see him there, so before I answered his questions, I asked him what he was still doing there. I thought he was leaving.

"Betty asked me if I wanted to stick around and work on my carving," he told me. "I decided to take her up on her offer."

We led the horses into the corral, and Buckley started grilling me about the lobo again while I took Hank's saddle and bridle off.

In the middle of it, I met Marie's friend, a woman named Teresa Tewa.

Teresa asked Marie where she was going in case she needed to get in touch with her.

"It's better if you don't know," Marie said. "If you need me, just let my parents know, and they'll get word to me."

"We better go," Betty said.

"Buckley's taking us in Gramps' camper," Hannah said.

"It's Buckley's now," Betty said.

Marie came over to me and gave me a hug. "Thanks for trying to help out with Dad."

"Well, I'm a believer now," I said. "I'll talk to him again and see if I can't persuade him to catch it."

I was also going to talk to Rand and try to make him a believer, too.

"Thanks." Marie started toward the camper, then stopped and turned around. "You're welcome to ride Hank while I'm gone."

Not likely, I thought, but I said, "Thanks."

Taw was sitting at the rickety table reading a magazine by the light of a hissing Coleman lantern. He looked up when I walked in and said, "You've been stalking."

I hadn't had a chance to get cleaned up. I sat down and told him about the lobo and about my conversation with Uncle John.

"I'm going to call Rand McKenzie tomorrow and try to convince him that there actually is a wolf here."

"You might want to hold off on that," Taw said. "At least until after you talk to John again."

"If it's really a Mexican wolf, Rand needs to know."

"I agree, but I still think you should talk to John first."

I didn't have the energy to argue with him. "I had no idea Uncle John was a trapper."

"He's been catching animals his whole life. When he was a young boy he caught hawks. The elders used the feathers for our ceremonies. John knew where a bird would land before the bird knew itself. When he got older he used this gift to catch coyotes and wolves. He started working for local ranchers and the word spread, and he was sent all over the country. I think he's sorry he caught them now, and he regrets teaching others the skill."

"Especially Earl."

Taw stood up. "I'm going to turn in."

I scrounged around for some food and found a can of beans and some piki bread. After I ate I lay in bed for a long time thinking about the dream I had had at Chaco Canyon. When Supeet said, *He needs your help,* I thought he meant Doc or Taw, but maybe he meant Uncle John. Uncle John had caught me with his left hand. Maybe I could help him use it again.

Once again I missed the sunrise. I probably would have stayed in bed longer had our single room not turned into an adobe oven. I wasn't surprised to see that Taw had already fled the inferno. I got dressed and went out expecting to find him on the roof, but he wasn't there.

I walked to the main plaza. No one was around. I

was about to go back to Taw's when I heard voices.

"Taw?"

"In the kiva," came the muted reply.

There was a ladder sticking out through the roof of the kiva. I walked over and looked down into the dark entrance.

"Join us," Taw said.

I climbed down. It was at least twenty degrees cooler in the kiva, which explained why he and the others were down there. The kiva was rectangular, and much bigger than I had expected. When my eyes adjusted to the dim light, I saw there were dozens of gruesome masks stacked along the walls. The masks represented different kachinas and were used in the Hopi ceremonial dances. I thought again of my dream.

Taw, Uncle John, Betty, Buckley, and a couple of other old roots I hadn't met before were sitting on the floor around the square sipapu in the stone floor. I sat down next to Taw.

"We're talking about the lobo," he said. "Tell us what you saw in the pasture yesterday evening."

When I finished they all looked at Uncle John.

"If the lobo allowed you to get that close, others might be able to do the same," he said. "If Jacob is willing to help me, I guess I'll try to capture it."

Marie was going to be very happy about this. "I'm willing," I said.

"Good, but I have some conditions." He leaned toward me. "The first is that if we catch the lobo, we will not put it in a cage. We will take it back where it belongs. We will take it back home."

"Do you mean Mexico?"

"Yes."

"They don't even know if there are any lobos left in Mexico," I said. "Not to mention the fact that it's probably illegal to take a wolf across the border and set it free without permits, which would be nearly impossible for us to get."

"I have a lot of contacts along the border, and Buckley has offered to smuggle the lobo across."

"Okay, let's say he gets the lobo across the border without getting arrested. Then what? Where will you let it go?"

"I know exactly where the last few lobos live in Mexico." Uncle John seemed to have an answer for everything.

"You also know how important the lobo would be for the captive breeding program," I said.

"I do," John said. "In fact, I caught two of the original lobos for the program. That's how your friend Rand knew my name."

"Don't you think we should at least tell him about the lobo?"

John shook his head. "This wolf has made its way across the border, skirted cities, towns, ranches, and roads. It worked hard and took great risks to get here. I will not be part of putting it into a cage. And we need to keep this absolutely quiet. If it gets out that I'm trying to capture the lobo, we'll have people following us all over Hopiland hoping to get it before we do. The last thing I want is to lead people to the wolf."

This made sense, but I was still uncomfortable about not using the wolf for the captive breeding program.

"I have a condition, too," Taw said.

We all looked at him.

"While Jake is helping you, John, I'll be staying at your place."

"Why?"

"He came down here to spend time with me," he said. I had a feeling this was not the only reason Taw wanted to stay there. I was sure his tools were coming with him.

"Fine." Uncle John stood up. "We'll need to get started right away. Jake, I want you to ride Hank over to the ranch."

"Hank?"

"You'll need him when you check the traps," John explained.

He and the others climbed up the ladder.

Hank was very surprised to see me again, but even more surprised when I tried to saddle him. Fortunately, Teresa heard me yelling at him and came to his rescue. She showed me how to put a saddle on.

"Hank's not going to be happy when you separate him from Heather."

"Should I take her with me?"

"It's up to you." The phone rang and Teresa ran back into her house to get it.

I decided that having two horses was twice as much trouble as one. I opened the corral gate and led him out by himself, then swung into the saddle.

"Giddyap."

He stiffened and stood as still as a saguaro cactus.

"Give me a break!"

Hank tried. I flew off the saddle, hitting the ground on my hands and knees. I got up immediately and grabbed his reins.

"Listen, you lunkhead!" I shouted. "I don't want to ride you any more than you want to be ridden, but I am going to ride you if it's the last thing I do!"

Apparently, Hank got the message, because he settled down as soon as we left Polacca.

We hadn't gotten very far into the desert when I saw a plume of dust rising up in the distance along the dirt road we were following. I turned Hank off to the side and waited for the truck to pass. It wasn't until it was fifty yards away that I realized it was Earl's truck. I thought about kicking Hank in the sides and making a run for it, but with my luck I would fall off. I held my ground. Earl slammed on his brakes and came to a skidding stop about ten feet away from us.

Hank's nostrils flared, and he started dancing around. "Easy, Hank. Don't dump me now."

Earl jumped out of his truck and stomped over to us without waiting for the dust to settle. I was happy to see that he didn't have his friends with him. "You're on my horse!" he shouted. Hank backed up a few paces. "Get off!"

Not for a million dollars, I thought. We stared at each other for a few moments, then Earl gave me his smile. "You don't happen to know where Marie is, do you?"

I didn't say anything.

"Look, I know I've been kind of a jerk, but I'm over it now. All I want to do is talk to her."

"I don't know where she is."

He made a grab for the reins. Hank saw it coming and backed out of reach. What a horse. "Are you going to get off, or do I have to pull you off?" He made another lunge for the reins, ripping them out of my hands. Hank reared, picking Earl off the ground like a fish on a line, slammed him back down, then whirled around and galloped away with me clinging to the saddle like a piece of lint. I looked back and saw Earl writhing on the ground, clutching his shoulder. I had an attack horse.

After a couple of miles Hank slowed to a walk so my guts could find their original location. He glanced back at me.

"Nothing better than starting the day off with a good brawl, hey, Hank?"

He whinnied.

When we reached the pasture where I had seen the lobo, I swung out of the saddle and tied Hank to the gate. I walked down to the southeast corner to check the carcass to see if the lobo had returned. The carcass was exactly where the lobo had left it. As I approached, two vultures flew off, but the flies and ripe smell remained.

"I thought you'd stop here," a voice said behind me.

I nearly jumped out of my shoes. It was Uncle John. He and Buckley stepped out from behind a tree about fifty feet from the carcass.

"What are you doing here?"

"Learning a little something about our lobo." He limped over. "And you?"

"I wanted to see if it had come back."

He looked at the carcass. "Fifty years ago the lobo would have returned. There would be nothing here but a pile of cracked bones. But the survivors have learned that revisiting a kill is a death sentence."

The camper was parked on the other side of the fence. "Where are Betty and Taw?"

"We dropped them at the house," Buckley said.

"I ran into Earl on the way here. He was looking for Marie."

"He better not come to the ranch," John said. "Betty has a shotgun. Now, get your mind off Earl. We have a lobo to catch." He picked up a stick and walked over to the carcass. "The lobo has been trapped at least twice before."

"How can you tell?"

"It's missing a toe on its right front paw and a partial toe on its left rear paw." He pointed to the tracks with the stick.

I took a close look at the faint impressions,

barely making out the missing toes. I looked over at the fence it had jumped with a sheep haunch in its mouth. "Doesn't seem to have slowed it down much."

"No," John said. "But being trapped twice before is going to make it very difficult to trap a third time."

"For Earl, too."

"He doesn't care if it's alive or dead. This gives him a lot more options than we have. We'll have to spend as much time trying to catch this lobo as it spends trying to avoid us. Are you ready for that?"

"Yes. But what about the possibility of there being more than one lobo? We heard two howling the other night."

"Forget that for now." He looked back at the ground. "I assume the wind was coming from the south when you made your stalk."

I nodded.

"And you stalked without clothes."

"Marie told you that."

Uncle John shook his head. "I haven't talked to Marie, and she didn't tell Buckley or Betty about it, either. I found the broken yucca and saw where you rolled on the ground. Did the lobo see you when you got close?"

"I don't think so, but it knew something was there."

"Is that when the truck came?"

I nodded.

He walked over to the exact spot where I had stood when I first saw the lobo. "The lobo ran before the truck arrived. You watched it jump the fence, then you stood right here until the truck passed." He pointed to the cigarette butt. "Earl's?"

"Yes," I said, amazed.

"Have you ever tracked an animal?"

"Not really."

"You'll start today. I want you to follow the lobo's prints as far as you can while there's light. Let's go, Buckley." He started walking to his truck.

"Where are you going?"

"We'll see you back at the house. When you lose the tracks, walk in widening circles until you pick them up again. It's all a circle, you know. Like that amulet you're wearing around your neck. One more thing. When you saw the lobo, was there enough light to see its eyes?"

"Yes."

"Did you see the fire there?"

There was something in the eyes, something I hadn't recognized before. "I'm not sure."

"You saw it," he said. "I can see it in your eyes now, and it wasn't there yesterday when I saw you at the house. When you get close enough to see the fire, you take some of it away with you. The fire is kindled only in wild wolves. You don't see this fire in caged wolves. A captive wolf is merely the smoke of what it once was. I've killed wolves, and put a number of them in cages, but I will not extinguish this lobo's fire. Not this one."

Uncle John and Buckley got into the camper and drove away.

t e n

I lost the lobo's prints on the other side of the fence, so I started circling as John had suggested. Over the next hour I saw a lot of tracks—rodent, rabbit, bird, snake, ant, scorpion— but no lobo prints. It was as if the lobo had jumped the fence and never come down. Why was Uncle John having me go through this? The tracks were almost a day old now, and the lobo was miles away and probably still moving.

I was about ready to give up when I saw a tuft of sheep's wool clinging to a cactus. There were bits of wool all over the pasture, but this one had blood on it. I spent the next half hour staring at every inch of ground within ten feet of the cactus and was finally rewarded with a perfect impression of the lobo's right front paw. Finding the next print was easy. I followed the tracks to the next fence, which the lobo had crawled under, dragging the haunch. I marked the spot, walked back and got Hank, then started all over again.

The lobo had traveled in a relatively straight line for nearly a mile, then turned left, which took me an hour to figure out. The tracks led me up a small rise. On top of the rise were several large flat rocks, big enough to park a semi-truck on. In the center of the largest rock was a piece of paper weighted down with a rock. I picked it up. There was a note scribbled on it: *"Not bad. Come to the ranch."*

Uncle John didn't send me after the lobo to learn something about the animal. He sent me so he could learn something about me.

When I got back to the ranch, I found John in the kitchen sitting at the table with a map spread out in front of him. I gave him the note and he stuck it in his shirt pocket without comment.

"Where is everyone?"

"They went into town to get food, since we might be holed up here for a while."

"You knew where the wolf had gone," I said.

He pointed to a red mark on the map. "Flat Rocks is the highest point within ten miles of the pasture. I figured the lobo would go there and look back at Earl's truck to see which direction it was going. When the lobo saw the truck heading east, it went west for at least a mile. I lost its tracks right about here." He marked the spot with a small red dot and wrote the date next to it.

"The red marks indicate places I know for certain the lobo has been. The green question marks on the map are places where reported sightings have been made. Can't rely on those, though. Wolves tend to step right out of people's imaginations when there's a rumor of one in the neighborhood."

"What does the map tell you about the lobo so far?"

"It makes a kill, then the next night it moves at least ten miles away for another kill, and on the third night it might return where it killed the first night and kill again, or it might go to into a new area where there have been no killings. In other words, no pattern. This lobo is going to be difficult to catch."

"Where do we begin?"

"In the wolf shed."

I followed him outside and across the yard. The double doors leading into the wolf shed were locked with a heavy chain and padlock. By the rust on the chain and the difficult time John had in getting the lock open, I could tell the shed had not been used in a while. He swung the doors open, and we were hit with a blast of rank air.

"Whew!" I staggered backward.

"Smells like one of my vials busted." If the stench bothered him, he didn't show it.

"Vials?" I was standing ten feet behind him, covering my nose with my hand.

"You'll see."

I followed him inside. "When's the last time you were in here?"

"Couple of years, at least. I didn't think I would ever use the shed again. Betty wanted to turn it into a studio for her carving, but we never got around to it. Glad we didn't now."

He turned the lights on and started to pin the map on the wall. I looked around. A workbench ran the length of one wall. Underneath it was a small refrigerator, which seemed to be still working, if the loud humming was any indication. On top of the workbench were boxes of springs, steel trap jaws, chains, and several canine skulls. Dangling over the bench were aluminum noose poles varying in length from two feet to five feet. I could see they were well used by the teeth marks in the plastic guards around the ends. A bookshelf was mounted above the bench and was crammed with books on trapping, tracking, and wildlife. I was going to like hanging around in the shed.

On the wall next to the bench was a double stainless steel sink. Above it was a cabinet with glass doors. I opened a door and found where the bad smell was coming from. There were several glass bottles with numbers written on them. One of the bottles was cracked. I nearly passed out from the stench. "This one's cracked," I gagged.

"Take it outside," John said. "Hurry! And don't get any on you. I'll bury it later."

I ran outside with the bottle and put it as far from the shed as I could without taking a breath. When I got back to the shed, I asked John what it was.

"Wolf attractant," he said. "The magic elixir."

"What's it made out of?"

"Do you remember what it said on the vial?"

"Matrix number eight."

"That's a beauty. Let's see, it's made out of wolf liver with the gall, dung, brain, urine, and a little bit of musk gland thrown in for good measure. Effective."

"And potent."

"That, too. About twenty drops will usually pull in every coyote within ten miles. Doesn't seem to work on wolves, for some reason. I'll show you the best way to use attractants when we make and set our traps."

109

On the wall next to the map were several photographs of John and others handling wolves. He came over and pointed to one of the men in the photos. "That's Flaco," he said. "He knows more about lobos than any man alive. If we catch this wolf, you might get a chance to meet him. He knows exactly where the last lobos live, and he'll know where to let this one go."

"He's your contact in Mexico?"

Uncle John nodded. "Give me a hand over here."

I helped him pull out a heavy footlocker from underneath the bench. He opened the lid. Inside, stacked in neat rows, were a couple dozen steel leghold traps. They were covered with thick grease to keep them from rusting.

"We'll use these," he said.

I picked one up. It was heavy and had a long chain with a sharp two-pronged hook on the end of it. "What's the chain for?"

"It's called a drag. When the wolf gets caught in the trap, it runs off. The hook eventually snags a tree or bush, and that's about as far as the wolf is going to get."

"Why not just anchor the chain to something when you set the trap?"

"Because it would be difficult to hide the chain that way. If a wolf sees the chain, it's not going to go anywhere near that trap. Another reason we let them drag it is that it's a bit easier on their legs. Whatever the chain snags on usually has some give to it.

"This trap is called a Number Four Newhouse. It's the trap that eliminated the wolf from most of its range. Now they use the trap and the trapping techniques perfected back then to help the handful of wolves still in the wild."

I tried to spread the hinged jaws, but I couldn't budge them.

"If you could open the jaws with your bare hands, that trap wouldn't hold a prairie dog. Bring the trap over to the bench."

John pulled out two C-clamps. "Cinch down the two springs with the clamps."

I did and the jaw flopped open.

"This round plate in the middle is called the pan. Underneath it is the trigger." He held the trap up so I could see underneath. "I can't set the trap one-handed. You'il have to do it."

I moved the small lever underneath the pan into the notch, then set the trap on the bench.

"Okay," John said. "Gently take the clamps off."

The jaws stayed wide open.

"When pressure is put on the pan, it releases the trigger and the jaws snap shut. Now for the tricky part. You want to make sure you never touch that pan when the trap's cocked. And if you value your fingers, keep them clear of the jaws." He picked the trap up with his good hand and set it on the floor as carefully as if he were handling a land mine, then went over and got a broom from the corner and handed it to me. "Go ahead."

I tapped the pan with the end of the handle, and the trap jumped off the floor, almost ripping the handle out of my hand.

"Wouldn't that break every bone in a wolf's foot?"

"It will bruise the foot, but it usually doesn't break bones."

"Then how did our lobo lose its toes?"

"I suspect it was caught with a trap that had heavier springs. The jaws might have sliced the toes right off, or they didn't check the trap soon enough and the lobo pulled its toe off trying to get out of the trap.

"Outside you'll find a fifty-gallon barrel on a stand. Pull it out into the yard, fill it with water, then get a good fire going under it. We've got to get these traps cleaned up. I want to make our sets tomorrow morning, if we can get everything ready by then."

"Sets?"

"A set is a group of traps in one area. If my hunches are right, we'll be making three sets tomorrow."

Uncle John came out of the shed after I had the fire going and put a scoop of lye into the barrel. "We're boiling the traps to get the grease and human scent off them."

I dropped the traps into the barrel one at a time like steel lobsters. When I finished, John reached into his back pocket and pulled out a pair of deerskin gloves.

"Try these on for size." They fit well. "That's the last time you handle those or any other trapping gear with your bare hands."

When the traps had boiled long enough, I fished them out with a long hook and hung them on a line in the wolf shed to dry. As I was carrying the last trap inside, the camper pulled up. Tied onto the top were a dozen two-by-fours, a stack of plywood, and other building material.

Taw and Buckley got out of the front seat. Uncle John limped out of the shed. "What's all this?" he asked.

"You can't expect me to just sit around while you're out catching your lobo," Taw said. "I want to do a little tinkering while I'm here."

Uncle John grunted. "Well, I hope you bought some food, too."

Betty emerged from the back. "Don't worry," she said. "We have enough food to last us a year." She sniffed the air. "What's that smell?"

"Never mind," Uncle John said. "It'll go away in about a month."

After dinner Uncle John and I put our gloves on and returned to the wolf shed. He had me rub beeswax onto the traps to keep them working smoothly. When we finished he had me adjust the triggers and put the traps into a canvas backpack. I took the pack out to the camper. When I returned he was wrapping bottles of attractant in cotton and putting them into a box. "We'll keep these separate," he said. "Don't want to stink up Buckley's new rig."

No kidding, I thought.

"One more thing to get ready." He unlocked a metal cabinet. Inside were several rifles. "Tranquilizer guns. Have you ever used one?"

I had tranquilized a jaguar in Brazil, an elephant in Kenya, and deer at the zoo. "A few times."

"I don't usually take them along," he said, pulling a rifle out. "But if you'd had one of these when you stalked the lobo, Buckley would be on his way to Mexico right now to see Flaco. I don't know if you'll get another chance like that, but you better carry this with you."

"If you don't tranquilize the wolf, how do you get it out of the trap?"

"With a noose pole. I'll show you how to do that later."

He put a fresh CO_2 cartridge into the rifle's air chamber, then had me load a couple of darts from the vials of tranquilizer he kept in the refrigerator.

"Tawupu and you will be bunking in the shed, if that's okay. Buckley will sleep in the camper. There's not much room in the house."

"No problem."

"I'll get Buckley while you put the rifle in the camper. There's a rifle rack in the cab."

The sun was just about down. Uncle John and Buckley came out of the house and walked over to the camper.

"You ready?" Buckley asked me.

"For what?"

"We're going for a little ride in the desert."

In the dark it was impossible for me to tell where we were, but Buckley seemed to know where we were going. After a while he pulled the truck off the road and headed across the desert, swerving around cactus, sage, and the larger rocks. Several miles later he stopped the truck and we got out.

"No talking," Uncle John whispered as we started out on foot. We ended up at Flat Rocks, where he had left the note. We climbed to the top and sat down. The night was so still, the only thing I could hear was our breathing. John stood. I started to get up, but Buckley put his hand on my shoulder and shook his head.

Uncle John took several deep breaths, then brought his good hand to his face and cupped it around his mouth. He took another deep breath, and when he exhaled . . . he howled.

The sound came from somewhere deep inside him. It was beautiful and frightening at the same time. A chill moved through my body like electricity. Uncle John was the second lobo.

When he finished he caught his breath, then howled again. The second howl was clearer than the first, and the third was clearer still. I waited for the fourth howl, but it didn't come from Uncle John. The howl cut across the desert from miles away, tentative at first, then strong and radiant.

I closed my eyes and listened. By the time the last

note faded, I was convinced that Uncle John was right about taking the lobo home. It didn't belong in a cage.

When I opened my eyes, I saw headlights coming toward us.

"Looks like I howled up more than the lobo," Uncle John said. "Let's get back to the camper."

When we got there, Earl was waiting for us.

"So, you heard the lobo, too," Earl said. "I knew it was hanging around Flat Rocks."

The real lobo was at least ten miles away, but of course none of us told Earl this.

Earl stared at Uncle John's left arm. "Heard about your stroke," he said, smiling. "That's a shame. Kinda hard to set traps with one wing. Never heard of a cripple catching a wolf."

I started to take a step toward him, but Uncle John stopped me with his right arm. "Let it go, Jake."

Earl laughed. "He's given you good advice, cousin." Earl looked off into the night for a few moments. "If you're thinking about putting traps in the ground, you might as well forget it. That lobo isn't going to be around long enough to step into one of them."

He started back toward his truck and stopped before he got in. "One more thing, old man. I'm going to find Marie and Hannah. And when I do . . . You probably heard the bounty is up to twelve hundred and fifty dollars now. Hannah and I can travel a long ways on that kind of money."

Uncle John didn't say one word on the way back to the ranch.

eleven

"Quietly," Uncle John whispered. "I don't want to wake your grandfather."

I got out of my sleeping bag and crawled around the pitch-dark wolf shed trying to find my clothes. It looked like I was finally going to see a sunrise over Hopiland. When I got out to the camper, Buckley was already behind the wheel, and Uncle John was sitting next to him.

"Better put your gloves on," Uncle John said as we took off.

The trapping gear rattled in the camper behind us—half a dozen large crates, noose poles, traps, first-aid kit (for the lobo), wolf attractant, shovels, rakes, trowels, and a lot of other stuff I couldn't identify. Sitting on the floor in front of Uncle John was a large grocery bag filled with food Betty had prepared for us.

Buckley followed Uncle John's directions through the dark morning for nearly an hour. "We'll stop here," he finally said. "Wait for sunrise." He poured two cups of hot coffee from the thermos, handed one to Buckley, then began outlining his strategy.

"From studying the map, the lobo appears to hole up during the day in one of three areas. My guess is that it knows better than to make a kill in the area it's hiding in. Can't be sure, of course, but I've picked what I think are the three most likely places for its hideout."

"How will we know where to set the traps?" I asked.

"We'll look for signs, but we may not find any. This lobo has had a lot of hard experience. Most lobos will use roads if there aren't people around, but our lobo doesn't seem to use roads even when one's handy. At least I haven't seen any prints on a road, but I have seen prints along the edges where it jumped across the road. It's almost as if the lobo has learned that its tracks will lead people to it."

He finished the last gulp of coffee. "We'll make three sets of several traps and see what happens. When we get more information, we may try putting traps in other areas, but for now we'll concentrate on the three areas I've chosen. Let's take a look around."

As the sun rose it cast the mesas and buttes above the desert in red and orange light. It was beautiful. I was determined not to miss a sunrise again.

Uncle John got the rifle out of the rack and slipped a tranquilizer dart into it. He handed it to me. "You never know, you might get lucky again. Buckley, you and Jake take this side of the road, and I'll take the other. What we're looking for are scats, tracks, scratch marks, or scent marks at the base of bushes or trees. If you see something, give me a holler."

I saw a lot of things, and each time I hollered John crossed the road, looked at my find, shook his head, and patiently explained what it was.

"Coatimundi scat. Too small for a lobo."

"Coyote scratch marks. See how narrow the marks are? Wolves have thick, blunt toenails."

"Could be a scent mark, but I don't think our lobo would mark this high up a tree unless it was carrying a stepladder with it. Probably a buck deer . . . about the right height for that."

We followed the road for quite a while. As the sun climbed, the back of my neck started to burn. I was beginning to doubt we would ever see a track when John shouted, "Take a close look around on your side. There should be some prints."

"Here's one," Buckley shouted back.

John came over and took a look. "It jumped right over the road. This is one cautious lobo. Get the traps."

I pulled the heavy pack out of the camper.

"I don't want to contaminate the real trap sites, so I'm going to show you how to set a trap right here in the road." He pointed to a spot about two feet from the camper. "I'll set a trap the best I can with my bum arm. I'll do it just like the real thing. Give me some room, but pay close attention, because you'll be setting the rest of the traps."

Buckley and I backed away a few paces.

Uncle John untied the end of a large plastic bag and pulled out a bundled animal skin. I had wondered what was in the bag. He rolled the skin out on the ground, hair side down. I couldn't see it very clearly upside down, but it looked a lot like a gray wolf pelt. A very big gray wolf, by the looks of it.

"Is that—or was that—a lobo?"

"Not a Mexican wolf. We don't grow them this big down here. A lobo weighs about sixty to eighty pounds. I trapped this wolf in Alaska a long time ago. Big male. Weighed well over a hundred pounds. I've used it as a drop cloth ever since. Most trappers use a plastic or canvas tarp nowadays. Some of the old timers use a cowhide. The important thing is to use some kind of drop cloth. On a hot day like today the cover will catch your sweat. A smart wolf can smell a drop of sweat in the dust twenty feet away several hours after it dripped from your brow. One whiff of human sweat and the wolf is outta here."

He picked up the trowel and stared at the ground for a long time. "I'm memorizing what it looks like. You can bet the lobo will remember. If it sees something out of place . . ."

"The wolf is outta here," I finished.

John laughed. "Right. When you walk away from a set, it should look like you were never there. Jake, open this trap for me."

I clamped the springs down, set the trigger, then removed the clamps and carefully handed it back to him.

He set the trap on the skin and started to dig, putting each scoopful of dirt into a shallow wooden box about a foot square with a screen bottom. The first hole was pretty deep. When he finished it, he coiled the drag chain into the hole, then covered the chain with dirt. It looked like the trap had taken root. The next hole was more shallow—a little deeper than the depth of the trap and in the same shape. Very gently, he placed the trap in the hole. "That's a good fit. Almost done."

He put a square piece of paper that had been soaked in beeswax on top of the trap to prevent dirt from fouling the trigger, then picked up the screen box and began sifting dirt back into the trap hole by shaking it.

When the trap was completely covered, he used the trowel to sprinkle bits of ground debris on top of the dirt. He inspected the set from different angles, gently nudging debris here and there until he was satisfied with how it looked.

"One more thing to do," he said. He reached into the box of magic elixir and pulled out a vial. "We're going to use number four." He opened the cap and dunked a small twig into the bottle and pulled it out. I could smell it from where I stood ten feet away. He stuck the twig in the ground near the trap, then moving backward on his knees, rolled the wolf pelt toward him, catching the extra dirt and tools in the soft hide. He stood up stiffly and stumbled forward when he put weight on his left leg. Buckley and I rushed forward to catch him.

"I'm okay," he protested. "I'm okay."

We let him go, but stayed close by.

Uncle John pointed at the ground. "What do you see, Jake?"

"It looks like you were never there."

"Good. Now follow me. Bring the gear."

We followed him about a hundred feet away. "With Buckley's hand wrapped like a mummy's and my useless arm, it's all up to you, Jake."

Uncle John pointed to a pinion tree about thirty feet in front of us. "You'll put your first trap right over there. See the scent mark at the base of that trunk?"

I saw a tiny smudge mark, barely darker than the rest of the bark. I wouldn't have even noticed it, much less guessed it was a scent mark.

"The lobo urinated there several times," Uncle John continued. "But not recently. We'll stand right here and watch. I don't want to contaminate these sets any more than we have to. It's all yours."

It took me at least three times longer to set the trap with two hands than it had Uncle John with one, and I didn't do it nearly as well. When I finished I rolled up the wolf skin and joined them.

"The next one will be easier," Uncle John said. "Before we leave here I want you to draw a little map. You'll be checking the traps every day, and I don't want the traps disturbed, so you'll have to

125

check them with binoculars from horseback. Draw your map from where you think you'll stand your horse." He gave me a stack of white index cards. "This is what I usually use. Easy to carry in your pocket."

I wrote Set #1 Trap #1 on the first card and sketched a rough map.

I set the next five traps with John talking me through each step. The second trap took me almost as long as the first, but by the fourth trap, I had started to get the hang of it. After we finished, John had me hide two wolf crates in the brush.

"Nothing worse than having a wolf in hand and no place to put it," he said.

About noon we loaded the gear into the truck and drove to the second area he had picked. After eating lunch and washing it down with a gallon of water, we walked along the sides of the road looking for lobo tracks.

Once again we found a spot where the lobo had jumped over the road. I set four more traps, drenching the wolf skin in sweat. I took off my T-shirt.

For the fifth trap, John led me to a couple of large cottonwood trees. I dug the hole, C-clamped the springs, set the trigger, and gently placed the trap.

As I turned to get the screen box, my amulet snagged the pan and the trap exploded from the hole like a striking rattler. I reeled backward, nearly rolling off the wolf pelt. Astonishingly, the trap seemed to follow me and thumped me on the chest.

Uncle John and Buckley doubled over laughing.

"That trap really came out of there," I said, not sure what they found so funny, but when I said it, they started laughing even harder.

Uncle John got down on one knee and tried to catch his breath. When he had recovered enough to speak, he wheezed, "That trap didn't fly out of the hole. You pulled it out! The jaws caught your necklace and when you jerked away, you yanked the trap right out of the ground. The look on your face . . ." Laughter overtook him again.

I felt around my neck, then looked at the trap. My leather thong was clamped in the steel jaws, and the amulet and jaguar tooth were gone. I started crawling around looking for them.

"What are you doing?" John asked. "You're contaminating the area."

"I don't care," I said frantically. "I need to find the amulet."

They started to help me. I found the tooth first, and I was relieved, but what I really wanted was the amulet. It felt strange not having it around my neck. I put the tooth in my pocket and continued to search.

"Here it is," Uncle John said.

It was right in the center of the trap hole. He stood up and handed it to me. I was thankful to have it back.

The final trapping area was nowhere near a road. We drove across the desert for several miles until we got to a deep, dry, twisting arroyo. We searched both sides and the bottom for a couple of miles, but saw no lobo signs. John was surprised and seemed a little disappointed, but he had me set three more traps there anyway. Before we left he had me hide the last two crates in the brush as I had at the other sites.

It was dark by the time we got back to the ranch. I stumbled into the wolf shed and fell asleep without even changing out of my filthy clothes.

t w e l v e

The next morning I was awakened by the sound of hammering. Bright sunlight streamed through the window above my sleeping bag. I was so tired and stiff from setting traps the day before, I didn't care that I had missed yet another sunrise.

I got dressed and went outside. Taw and Buckley were on the roof of the house, pounding away. Uncle John was down below, looking up at them with a helpless look on his face. I walked over to him.

"They're ruining my house," he said.

"I doubt it. Taw's pretty handy with a hammer. Remember, he used to build skyscrapers."

"My house is hardly a skyscraper." Uncle John looked me up and down. "How do you feel?"

"Sore."

"Well, today you and Hank are on your own." He

walked over to the porch and came back with a noose pole and handed it to me.

I wasn't looking forward to getting into the saddle. "What if the lobo is in a trap?"

"Then you'll have to crate it and ride back and get me."

An empty crate was sitting next to the camper. "But I've never . . ."

"You've seen your father crate a wolf. Right?"

"Yes, but . . ."

"There's nothing to it." He gave a short whistle. His old cattle dog got up stiffly from its corner on the porch, waddled out to us, and flopped down in the dust, exposing its belly.

"This is Dyna," John said, squatting down and scratching her. "Short for Dynamite. We'll use her as our stand-in lobo. The real lobo might put up more of a fuss than Dyna, so you'll have to use your imagination a bit for this demonstration."

I looked down at Dyna. Her mouth was hanging open. She had only three teeth left. No kidding, I thought.

"Go ahead and put the noose around her neck and tighten it."

I did and the mild mannered Dyna transformed into her namesake. She snarled, barked, snapped, pushed, and dragged me halfway across the yard. Taw and Buckley had grandstand seats and laughed so hard they nearly fell off the roof. John walked over and took the pole from me. Dyna didn't care that her master was now at the end of the pole. If she got out of the noose, she was going to kill both of us.

John lay the noose handle on the ground and put a foot on it, pinning Dyna's head to the ground. Dyna twisted and snapped at the pole. "Sorry about this, old friend," John said. "But you're the only wolf we have handy." Eventually, Dyna stopped struggling, but her eyes told an entirely different story.

"There are two ends of a wolf you have to watch out for," John said. "One end has teeth." He looked at Dyna's mouth. "Normally. And the other end is messy. The only end you have to worry about is the toothed end." He pulled a three-foot strip of gauze out of his pocket. "You'll use this as a muzzle."

Dyna started to struggle again, but it was fruitless with her head pinned to the ground. John tied a loop in the strip of gauze. Holding the two ends, he swung the loop over Dyna's muzzle and pulled the ends in opposite directions, cinching the jaws closed. He passed the two ends under the lower jaw, then brought the ends up behind the ears and tied a bow.

"With the tooth end secure, you can take the trap off." He handed me the pole, brought the crate over, and upended it with the door open. "All you have to do now is grab the lobo's hind legs or the base of its tail and the scruff of its neck and lower it into the crate tail first. Go ahead."

I grabbed Dyna's hind legs and the scruff of her neck and picked her up. She was a lot heavier than I expected. I lowered her into the crate.

"Before you release the noose, take the muzzle off by pulling on one of the ends." He pulled the end and the muzzle fell off. "That's all there is to it."

I released the noose and shut the crate door. I thought it might be best to leave Dyna in the crate until she cooled off, but John let her out. Before she could bite us or run away, he reached into his pocket and gave her a dog biscuit. Dyna wolfed it down and acted like nothing had happened. John made me noose, muzzle, and crate Dyna half a dozen times more. Dyna wasn't thrilled with the role as stand-in lobo, but she tolerated it for the biscuit at the end.

"It's going to take you all day to check traplines on horseback. You better gather your gear and get moving."

I went back into the wolf shed to get my gloves and remembered that the amulet and jaguar tooth were still in my pocket. I looked around for something to tie them around my neck, but I couldn't find anything. Reluctantly, I left the tooth and amulet on the workbench, afraid I might lose them while I was out checking the traps.

Hank was actually excited to see me. He trotted over to me and nickered. I saddled him and loaded everything I thought I would need, including the tranquilizer rifle. We headed out to the first trapline.

As I rode, I sorted through my pile of trap maps, trying to visualize where each trap had been set. I named the first set of traps Pinion because of the two pinion trees there. I named the second set of traps Cottonwood, because the trap that nearly snapped my nose off was in front of two large cottonwood trees. And the third set of traps I called Twisting Gulch because of the deep arroyo snaking its way through the area.

It took us almost two hours to get to Pinion, with only one stop on the way—Hank insisted on getting a long drink of water from a sheep trough we passed. On the way, I kept my eyes glued to the ground looking for lobo signs, but I didn't see any.

I found all the traps at Pinion without much problem. As John instructed, I stayed on Hank and checked the traps from a distance through binoculars so I wouldn't contaminate the sites. As far as I could tell, none of the traps had been disturbed.

The traps at the Cottonwood set were not as easy to find. The problem we'd had with the amulet had distracted me. The maps I'd drawn didn't make sense. I nearly walked Hank right into one of the traps. The only thing that prevented this was Hank getting a whiff of the wolf attractant and backing out of there like there was a lobo snapping at his nose. I thought about moving the trap, but Uncle John hadn't explained why he put the traps where he had, so I didn't know where to move it to. It took me more than two hours to find all of the Cottonwood traps.

We got to Twisting Gulch just before sunset, and like the other areas, none of the traps had been touched. John had told me not to be surprised if we didn't catch the lobo right away. He had said it can take weeks and sometimes months to lure a wolf in.

On the way back to the ranch I decided it might be easier to spend a night out every other day. I could leave the ranch early in the morning, spend the night near Twisting Gulch, then check the traps in reverse order the next morning. This would put me back at John's by early afternoon every other day to hang out with Taw.

It was almost ten when I opened the last gate

before we reached the ranch. Halfway across the pasture I heard Taw, Uncle John, and Buckley laughing. It was deep, loud, breath-snatching laughter from two old friends and one new friend. Hearing them enjoying themselves made me very happy. I stopped and listened for a while, afraid to approach the house and take the moment away from them.

I got off Hank and led him to the corral. I took my time brushing him out and putting the gear in the wolf shed. I found the three old roots sitting on the front porch in rockers as though they had spent their evenings this way for the past fifty years.

"Did you catch that lobo?" Uncle John asked.

"No, sir, I didn't." I told them about my day, including how I had almost walked Hank into the trap at Cottonwood. "Should I move it tomorrow?"

"Did you get off Hank?"

"No."

"Shouldn't be a problem then."

Betty came out carrying a bowl of steaming lamb stew and a plate of hot biscuits. "I assume you're hungry."

"I am." I sat down on the top step and started to eat. Dyna crawled out a few inches from her corner. I dipped a biscuit in the stew and tossed it to her. She gulped it down without chewing and waited for the next one, which wasn't long in coming. After what I had done to her earlier, she deserved every biscuit on the plate, but Betty put an end to my peace offerings.

"She's had hers, now you eat yours," she scolded.

"Betty talked to Pete today," Taw said.

"He left a message at the community center for you to call," she explained. "I called him back, knowing you weren't going to be near a phone for a while. He said he talked to a friend of your father's in Brazil named Buzz who said it was too late to stop your dad from coming up here. He's already on his way, but it will take a while for him to arrive."

Doc would have to go by boat to the nearest town that had an airplane, which could take a week or more. I was actually glad he was on his way. I wanted him to see for himself how well Taw was doing. He would also be able to help us catch the lobo if we didn't catch it before he arrived.

"I picked up the latest lobo rumors, too," she said. "Two lambs were killed near Second Mesa."

"But it could have been a coyote that did the killing," Uncle John added. "Since the lobo got here, everyone seems to have forgotten that the lobo's little cousin has been taking livestock here for hundreds of

136

years. Now, every time a sheep or cow is killed it's the lobo. I like where the traps are set for now."

I told him about my plan to spend every other night at Twisting Gulch to save time. Taw and Uncle John didn't like the idea, saying it wasn't safe for me to be alone in the desert at night.

"Especially with Earl running around," Uncle John said.

I was about to remind them that I had wandered across Kenya on my own and it had been a lot more dangerous there, when Buckley came to my defense. "I wouldn't mind setting the camper up where Jake wants to camp. In fact, I would enjoy it."

"What about your plan?" Taw asked.

"Do we have to do it every night?" Buckley asked. "I could come in every other day when Jake is back here."

"What plan?" I asked.

Taw chuckled. "We were talking about Earl's chances of getting this lobo, and Buckley came up with the idea of leading him astray by having John let out some well-placed howls."

John smiled. "In the wrong places, of course. I never took Earl out howling, so he doesn't know anything about this technique for finding wolves. Last night he drove right to my howl. I can howl him into little circles. And that would sure be fun."

"Could we do it every other night?" Taw asked.

"Actually, it might be better that way. Less chance of him catching on to us."

"So, I can camp with Buckley at Dry Gulch?" I asked.

"It's okay with me," Taw said.

"You'll need to set up your camp a long way from that arroyo," Uncle John said. "This lobo moves around at night. You being out there could affect where the lobo goes and where it stays, so you have to be careful."

"I think I know a good spot," Buckley said.

Betty went back inside and I ate my food, sneaking Dyna a couple more biscuits. When I finished I got up and told them I was going to sleep.

"I'll be along soon," Taw said.

"You might want this." Uncle John pulled something out of his pocket. It was the amulet and jaguar tooth strung on a new leather thong, but what pleased me even more was that he was holding it out to me with his left hand. The hand was trembling with the effort. "Started working again late this afternoon," Uncle John said, straining to keep the hand raised. "It has a long way to go, but it's good to have it back."

I put the amulet around my neck.

"Try to keep it clear of those jaws."

"What jaws?" Taw asked.

Buckley and Uncle John started laughing again.

thirteen

A week passed and the traps still lay undisturbed beneath the ground like dormant seeds.

Buckley and I set up our semipermanent camp in a small stand of trees about five miles beyond Twisting Gulch. There was plenty of wood for our campfire, and in back of the site was a small rise with a short spire on top that was easily climbed for a spectacular view. On each trip we brought out a few things from the ranch to make the camp more comfortable. I told Uncle John that if the lobo didn't step into one of the traps soon, we would have a nicer place than his.

"Don't count on it," he said.

He and Taw were making a lot of progress on the house. Each time I returned, something new was fixed. They had replaced the window glass, repaired the broken steps to the porch, and were working on patching the adobe outside the house, but there was still a lot to do.

Uncle John's left side got stronger every day, but it wasn't because of the lobo. It was because of Taw. He wouldn't tolerate Uncle John feeling sorry for himself or let him get out of work because of his problem. At first Uncle John resented Taw egging him on, but the resentment faded as his strength returned.

The lobo struck three times during the week. Uncle John put more red dots on the map, but he still liked where our traps were and saw no reason to move them or to put in another set of traps.

Every other night we went out howling. Earl's truck was easy to spot on the desert with the row of spotlights on the roll bar. Uncle John would howl him up, and the four of us would jump into the camper and drive off laughing long before he got near us.

On camp nights, I usually got to Twisting Gulch by late afternoon. After checking the traps I would ride over to a well not far from the arroyo, wash up, fill my water bags, then head over to camp. Uncle John gave me a pair of hobbles for Hank's front legs, so he wouldn't wander too far during the night. He and I were getting along like old friends now. After brushing him out I would let him go, then join Buckley, who always had dinner cooking on the fire. Before sunset we climbed the spire behind camp and sat there until nightfall, scanning the desert with binoculars, hoping to see the lobo. The rest of the evening was spent near the fire talking about Buckley's days as a biologist in the Pacific Northwest and what Doc was doing in Brazil.

Buckley's hand had healed enough for him to take the bandage off. As we talked he whittled away on a kachina. I asked what kind of kachina he was carving.

"A wolf kachina, of course," he said.

I had seen the untouched ground over the traps so many times, I had just about given up hope of the lobo stepping into one of our traps. Then, on my tenth trip back to the ranch, I came across a sprung trap at Cottonwood. No lobo, but its prints were all over the place. Either the trap missed, or the lobo had pulled out of it. I picked up the trap and looked at the jaws for blood or hair, but there was no sign of either.

I was excited and wanted to run back to the ranch and tell Uncle John, but I made myself check the rest of the traps. I'm glad I did, because the next trap over was pulled out of the ground, too, and so were the third and fourth traps. I took a close look at the ground at the fourth trap and saw nail marks where it looked like the lobo had actually dug the trap out. I rechecked the first three sprung traps and found the same thing. It was as if the lobo knew the traps were there and in a rage had gone down the line and yanked them out by their drag chains. I didn't know if I should reset the traps or not, so I took them back to the ranch after I checked the traps at Pinion.

Taw and Uncle John were stringing new barbwire in the sheep pasture when I rode up. Uncle John took a close look at each of the traps in the bright afternoon light.

"I think you're right," he said. "The lobo dug them out. I've seen it happen before. No other traps disturbed?"

"No."

He looked at the sun. "Do you think you have time to get back to Cottonwood and reset these?"

"I think so. Where should I put them?"

"In the same holes the lobo dug them out of. No, wait. On second thought, let's have Buckley drive us out there, which will save time, and we'll do a blind set."

"What's that?"

"We'll put these traps in the same holes, then set

143

two more traps nearby without any attractant. Wolves sometimes get careless and bumble into one. We'll see if our lobo has ever run into that trick."

Taw came with us. It turned out he knew Cottonwood well. "My father grazed his sheep here," he said. "Remember, John?"

"I remember."

"We used to climb these cottonwoods when we were kids. We were going to build a house right here, and . . ." Taw stopped and looked at John apologetically.

"It's all right, Tawupu," Uncle John said quietly. "Mary loved this spot, too. We all did, but that was a long time ago." He squatted down and looked at the ground where the trap had been. It was the same hole he had found my amulet in. "We better get to it. We have a lot of work before sunset."

Uncle John told me to put the original trap back in the same hole. "I'll set the other two," he said.

"You sure you're up to it?" Taw asked.

"Shut up, you old root," Uncle John snapped.

It took us a couple of hours to set the traps. Uncle John used a different elixir, hoping the new scent might entice the lobo to return.

f o u r t e e n

First thing the next morning, I checked the
Pinion traps, then galloped to Cottonwood
to see if John's trick had worked. It hadn't.
The area still looked as if we had never been there.

And there were no changes over the next several
days until the morning I caught the coyote.

I had gotten a late start because Uncle John and
Taw needed some help readjusting the solar panels on
the roof of the house. I got to Pinion about ten in
the morning and saw that one of the traps was missing. At first I thought we had the lobo, but when I
looked at the tracks, I saw that they were too small
and there were no missing toes. The drag marks from
the chain were easy to follow across the desert. The
coyote had pulled the trap for a quarter mile before
the hook snagged on a sage bush. As soon as the coyote saw me, it tried to run away, but the trap and
chain held fast.

I grabbed the noose pole and jumped off Hank, afraid the coyote might hurt itself trying to get away. It gave me a token snarl and halfheartedly bit at the noose as I put it around its neck and pinned its head to the ground. The trap had grabbed it by a single toe. The toe was swollen, but it didn't appear to be broken.

In my hurry I had forgotten to take the gauze for a muzzle. I didn't want to let the coyote go again, so I used the bandanna around my head to muzzle it, hoping it would hold long enough for me to get the coyote's toe out of the trap. I had also forgotten the clamps for the springs.

"I guess we're both learning some lessons today," I told the coyote.

There was a small gap in the jaws where they held the toe. I used my knife to pry the jaws apart just enough to get the toe out. In the process the blade snapped in two, but at least the toe was free. Other than a swollen toe, the coyote looked fine. Its buff-colored fur had shed out in the summer heat. The coyote watched every move I made with its alert yellow eyes. With my foot still on the pole pinning the coyote's head, I slowly reached for one of the ends of the bandanna tied behind its long ears. I yanked the end and the bandanna peeled off the coyote's jaws. I stood up and pulled the release on the end of the pole and gently removed the noose from around its neck. I expected the coyote to jump up and run away, but it just lay there panting and staring at me as if it didn't know it was free. I took a couple of steps backward. The coyote lifted its head, looked around, then jumped up and took off. Within a few seconds I couldn't see it anymore.

The whole process hadn't taken more than five minutes, and I was happy with the way I had handled the coyote, but I wasn't fooling myself. The lobo, if we caught it, would weigh four times as much as the coyote, and would be a lot more difficult to get out of a trap and into a crate.

I reset the trap and headed to the Cottonwood set.

When I got there I found that the traps we had set near the trees had been uprooted and were nowhere to be seen. At first I thought the lobo had returned and dug the traps up, but if that was the case, where were the traps? Certainly the lobo had not stepped into all three of them and dragged them off. A gust of wind blew toward us, and Hank started dancing around, making it difficult for me to focus the binoculars on the site. I told him to knock it off, but he was too nerved up to listen. He hadn't acted this way since the afternoon we'd encountered the lobo in the pasture. I swung off and tied him to a bush. I pulled the tranquilizer rifle out of the scabbard, made sure it was loaded, then started walking toward the cottonwoods. Halfway there, another gust of wind hit the trees, and I heard an odd clinking sound. I stopped and looked up. About twenty feet up I saw the three traps hanging from branches like grim Christmas tree ornaments. I looked at the ground and saw a boot print. When we'd set the traps, none of us had been wearing cowboy boots. Someone had pulled the traps and thrown them up into the trees.

I looked around the site and found the stick they had used to trigger the traps. One end was scarred where the jaws had snapped around it. I saw the lines in the dust where they had dragged the stick looking for the traps. My first thought was that Earl had been here, but almost everyone in Hopiland wore cowboy boots. It could have been anyone. But then there was Hank's reaction as we approached the trees. He wasn't fond of Earl, and he might get nervous if he picked up Earl's scent.

I climbed the tree and got two of the traps out of the branches, but I couldn't dislodge the third one. There was no point in resetting them here. The area was completely contaminated, and whoever pulled the traps might come back again.

I thought about riding back to the ranch right away and telling John what had happened, but I decided to check the other traps first and have Buckley drive me back, which would be faster. I found another trap that had been pulled. I looked around for it, but couldn't find it.

As I approached Twisting Gulch, I had a feeling I was being watched. I tried to shrug it off, thinking it was just paranoia from having the traps pulled, but Hank seemed to sense something, too. Instead of plodding steadily forward like he normally did, he was looking around a lot and throwing his head. Maybe my nervousness was running down through the reins and setting him on edge. I took a couple of deep breaths and tried to calm myself, then patted him on the neck and tried to convince him that things were just fine.

The first two traps at Twisting Gulch were intact. When I got to the third trap, Hank started dancing around again, but the trap was in place, and I didn't see any boot prints in the dust.

At the fourth trap, Hank reared up on his hind legs just as I was bringing the binoculars to my eyes. As I fell, I heard a loud bang. I hit the ground flat on my back, and all the air rushed out of my lungs. There was another loud bang. Hank fell to his knees, then flopped over on his side and started kicking. I watched in horror as his legs stiffened, then relaxed. He let out one final agonized sound. Then everything went quiet. I lay there for a few seconds trying to catch my breath and make sense out of what had just happened. When I had recovered enough to move, I crawled over to Hank and saw the blood still pumping through the gaping hole in his side. His eyes were wide open, staring at nothing. I tore my shirt off and tried to stanch the bleeding even though I knew he was dead. Another bang sounded, and the bullet hit the dirt three feet away from me. I dove behind Hank and curled up between his legs. Three more shots rang out, one after another, each sending a shudder through Hank's body as they struck home. The shots infuriated me. I wanted to jump up and tear the shooter into little pieces, but I kept my head and stayed hunkered down.

Aside from Hank, the only cover was a hundred yards away in the arroyo. There were another two shots, and I realized by where they hit that the shooter could just as easily have put one of the bullets into me. He was playing with me, and there wasn't a thing I could do about it.

Then I heard the howl, but it wasn't a wolf. It was a human trying to imitate a wolf and not succeeding. It had to be Earl. He must have figured out the howling game. An engine started in the distance.

I found my blood-soaked canteen tied to the saddle and took a long drink, then made a dash for the arroyo and jumped down into it. I either had to find a good hiding place or make my way to our camp and find Buckley. I decided to try to make it to camp. I needed to warn him that Earl was out here with a rifle.

I ran down the arroyo for a couple of miles before I had to stop and catch my breath. As I rested with my hands on my knees, I heard a horn honking, and the sound was getting closer. I looked around for a place to hide. There was none. Earl wouldn't be able to get his truck across the gulch. I began clambering up the opposite side, and hoped the fading light would prevent him from getting a good shot at me. When I reached the top, I started running. The horn was blaring right behind me, but I didn't turn to look.

"Jake!"

I stopped and turned. It was Buckley.

"Did you see Earl?" I asked. We were speeding across the desert toward Uncle John's.

"No. I heard the rifle shots and jumped in the camper and found Hank lying out there. I figured you took cover in the arroyo. You think Earl shot Hank?"

I told him about the howling.

When we got out of the camper at Uncle John's, I heard a horse nicker in the corral. I ran over to the fence. It was Heather. Marie had returned to Hopiland.

f i f t e e n

They were all sitting at the kitchen table when Buckley and I walked in.

"Jake!" Marie jumped up from the table smiling and started over to me. Because of the news I had, I couldn't return her smile. She stopped about halfway, and her expression turned from happiness to confusion.

"What happened?" Uncle John asked.

I told them about the traps first, not wanting to broach the really bad news right off.

"I was afraid something like that might happen," Uncle John said. "We could reset the traps. But the real problem is that someone else has figured out that the lobo might be using the Cottonwood site. I was hoping we would have the lobo before it occurred to anyone."

"There's another problem," I said. "Someone shot Hank."

Marie looked as if she hadn't heard me correctly. "What did you say?"

"When I was checking the traps at Twisting Gulch, someone shot Hank out from under me. He's dead."

They all just stared at me.

"He's dead?" Marie went back to the table and sat down.

I filled in the details.

"Earl," Marie said with more sadness than anger. She stood up. "Well, I'm going to the tribal police and tell them. Can I use the camper, Buckley?"

"Hold on, Marie," Uncle John said. "Let's stay calm. There's more at stake than your horse."

"Like what?" she asked.

"The lobo."

"I don't know what that—"

"If we go to the police, they'll want to know what we were doing out there. They'll go out and look at Hank. When they hear I set traps out there, everyone on Hopiland will know. Twisting Gulch will be crawling with people. If the lobo is there, it will either get shot, or it will move and we'll have to start all over again."

Marie closed her eyes and took a deep breath, visibly trying to calm herself. "So, what do you want to do?"

"I want to go out there tomorrow morning."

"And do what?"

"I'm not sure yet."

Marie walked with me to the wolf shed.

"I'm really sorry about Hank," I said. "We were getting along so well."

"He was a good horse." She stopped suddenly. "I can't believe that I didn't even ask if you were all right."

"I'm fine."

"You could have been hurt."

I could have been killed, I thought. We stood outside the shed for a few minutes, neither one of us knowing what to say about Hank. I broke the awkward silence by asking where Hannah was.

"I left her at Rand's."

"How's that going?"

"They're wonderful people. Rand's wife, Sandra, has been great, and Hannah is glued to Nicole. Won't leave her alone. But Nicole doesn't seem to mind."

"I'm glad that's working out. Guess I'll go in and go to sleep."

"Before you do I want to thank you for helping my dad. I can't believe how well he's doing. He's like a different person, thanks to you."

"Thanks to Taw," I said.

✳ ✳ ✳

Taw and Betty stayed at the ranch. Uncle John was in no hurry to get to Twisting Gulch. He stopped at Pinion, and while Marie and I checked the traps, he walked around looking for lobo signs. When we got to Cottonwood, he had us check the traps that were still in the ground. We met him at the two cotton-woods. He was squatting down looking at the ground.

"Cowboy boots," Marie said.

"Let's check the other traps."

When we got to Twisting Gulch, we could see Hank from a mile away. John had Buckley stop the truck long before we got to the carcass.

"You took cover under his belly?" he asked.

"Yeah."

He looked around some more, then had Buckley drive us north of where Hank lay.

"Where are you going?" Marie asked.

"I just want to check something out."

He had Buckley drive up a small rise with a stand of trees growing on top. We got out of the truck again and followed him over to the trees. Underneath the trees were more boot prints and five spent rifle shells. He picked them up and put them in the pocket of his overalls.

As we approached Hank, I could see that something was different, but I couldn't tell what it was until we were about fifty feet away. Buckley saw it at the same time and slammed on the brakes and turned off the engine. We stared through the windshield. Marie was in the back of the camper. "What is it?" she called through the rear window.

I pointed at the carcass. Hank's belly had been torn open, and a string of intestine was lying on the ground. I looked back at Marie, she didn't flinch.

"The lobo might have just made its first mistake," Uncle John said. "If my guess is right, it ate a meal in the area where it hides during the day. The temptation was just too great for it to resist."

We got out of the truck and walked over to Hank. Uncle John was right. The lobo's prints were all over the place. We followed the tracks from where Hank lay to the edge of the arroyo.

"I want you to wait up here for a bit," Uncle John whispered. "I need to check something out. Go back to the truck and don't make any noise."

"Dad, are you sure—"

"Go back to the truck, honey. I'll be fine." He started down the steep side of the arroyo before I could ask him what was going on.

We walked back to the truck. If I'd known the lobo was going to feed on Hank, I would have stayed and tried to get a tranquilizer dart into it.

Marie and I sat in the truck talking quietly. Buckley sat on the bumper working on his kachina. Marie wanted to know everything that had happened since she left Hopiland. She had to stifle her laughter when I told her about the amulet setting the trap off. I was happy to see her laugh.

John returned about forty-five minutes later, covered in sweat and dust. He said, "If you don't mind, Marie, I'd like to set a couple of traps near Hank."

"You think it will go back to the carcass?" I asked.

"To tell you the truth, I'm beginning to think we'll never catch this lobo in a trap, but it would be foolish not to set a couple there."

I started to get the gear together, but Uncle John stopped me. "How are you feeling, Jake?"

"Fine," I said, not sure what he was getting at.

"Rested?"

"Sure. Why?"

"How good of a shot are you with that tranquilizer rifle?"

"I don't know. Fair, I guess."

"Where's the rifle?"

It took a little effort to get the rifle out from the scabbard underneath Hank, but I managed to pull it out. It didn't appear to be damaged.

"Follow me," Uncle John said. "And keep your voices down."

We followed him about half a mile along the edge of the twisting arroyo.

"Have you ever hunted from a stand?" he whispered.

I shook my head.

"It's different than stalking an animal, but it can be just as difficult. Instead of going after the animal, you wait for the animal to come to you. See that hollow in the other side?" He pointed.

Directly across from us, about ten feet up from the arroyo bottom, was a small area where the bank sloughed off, forming a small cave about three feet deep.

"I want you to camouflage yourself and sit in that hollow for . . ." he looked at his watch, "about five hours or so. Do you think you can do that?"

"Sure, but—"

"I think the lobo is going to come down this arroyo about sunset along our side. You'll have one chance to put a dart into it."

"But we checked the bottom and didn't see any tracks."

"The lobo's not using the bottom," he said. "It's

using the sides, jumping from outcrop to outcrop. If my hunch is right, the lobo is in the arroyo right now waiting for the sun to go down, and if we're lucky, it's going to pass right below us. Can you hit it from across the arroyo?"

It would be about a twenty-five- or thirty-foot shot at a moving target. "I don't know," I admitted.

"Well, I want you to try. It might be our last chance. I think the lobo is going to leave this area soon. There's been way too much activity around here. It's going to find a quieter spot."

"Can I borrow your cane, Buckley?"

"Sure."

Uncle John stuck the cane into the ground right next to the edge. "You'll have to take plenty of water, because it's going to be hot. Once you're in the hollow, I don't want you to move."

I looked at the cane in the ground, wondering why he had stuck it there.

"This is your marker," he said. "You'll have to cross the arroyo up ahead, then double back on the other side until you get to Buckley's cane. You should be able to jump into the hollow from the top. Try not to disturb anything when you get in there. The lobo will know if something's out of place.

"In the meantime, we'll set the traps around

Hank, then find a good spot to wait. After you dart the lobo, give us a holler. We'll help you look for it."

I carried a gallon of water in one hand and the rifle in the other as I made my way back along the edge of the arroyo. Uncle John didn't explain why he was so confident that the lobo would pass by the hollow. When I asked him, all he said was that it was a hunch. I walked at least a mile and a half up from the cane before I found a good place to cross over.

When I reached the cane on the other side, I found a cactus with thick arms and broke a couple off. I smeared cactus juice on my skin and rolled in the dust. I was wearing a pair of shorts that were a pretty good color match with the surrounding dust, so I left them on. I smeared juice on the rifle as well and carefully covered it with dust.

I looked over the edge at the hollow, wishing I had thought to bring a rope to lower the rifle and my water jug down before I climbed into it. I leaned over the edge as far as I could and dropped the rifle, butt end first, into the hollow. I wasn't so lucky with the water jug. It bounced when it hit and landed in the bottom of the arroyo just above where I'd be sitting.

I lowered myself into the hollow and looked at

the jug. It was like a white neon arrow pointing up at me. If I jumped down to get it, I would have to walk down the arroyo until I could find a place to climb back up, fouling the bottom with my footprints and scent. As I leaned over, debating what I should do, a handful of dirt spilled from the edge and hit the jug. I had my solution. I'd bury my mistake. I wouldn't have any water to drink, but at least the arrow would be gone.

It took me more than an hour to cover the jug. When I dumped the last handful of dirt over the white cap, I was so thirsty I wanted to jump down and suck every last drop from the jug. I sat back in the hollow, trying to think of other things besides my thirst. I took hold of my amulet and closed my eyes. After a few minutes my thirst seemed to lessen.

I had the rifle resting across my knees. If the lobo came from my right, as John predicted, I would let it pass me before I raised the rifle to my shoulder. The arroyo took a sharp bend to my left. I'd have one chance to get a dart into the lobo's haunch before it disappeared around the corner. The shot would have to be perfect.

About an hour after I got settled, I heard the camper start and drive away.

I waited.

s i x t e e n

I decided that I much preferred stalking an animal to waiting for it to come to me. In a stand, or a sit, like I was in, the only decision I had to make was whether or not to scratch my face and risk removing some of the dust that covered me. When my legs started to cramp, I had to look up and down the arroyo to make sure the lobo wasn't coming before I moved them to a more comfortable position. It was the longest five hours I had ever spent.

As the sun got lower, the shadows in the arroyo began to lengthen. Suddenly, I saw something moving on my right. It was the lobo, and just as Uncle John said, it was using the bank as its trail. It moved slowly, jumping from one outcrop to the next as nimbly as a mountain goat. When it landed it stood on the ledge for a few moments, gauging its next jump before taking it.

I didn't dare raise the rifle as it was coming toward me. I stayed perfectly still and watched as it landed on a ledge directly across from me. It stood there for several seconds, looking around and sniffing the air as if it knew something wasn't right. I didn't breathe. The lobo jumped to the next ledge.

I raised the rifle to my shoulder in slow motion, then pointed the metal site at the ledge I thought it would land on next. It jumped. I gently squeezed the trigger.

At the same instant I fired the dart, a sharp bang echoed through the arroyo, followed by another. The lobo leaped off the bank and hit the bottom running, disappearing around the bend. I wasn't the only one hunting the lobo. I jumped out of the hollow and fell onto my hands and knees. My legs were numb and I had trouble standing.

I looked up. Someone was running along the edge in front of me following the lobo. I managed to get up and stumble down the arroyo. As I came around the bend, I saw Earl sliding down the bank about a hundred feet in front of me. He glanced at me, but didn't seem surprised that I was there. When he got to the bottom, he ran a few steps, then stopped. The lobo was in front of him, making its way unsteadily along the bottom. I must have got it with the dart and the drug was taking effect. Or Earl had wounded it. Earl braced one of his boots on an old snag and raised his rifle to his shoulder.

I shouted, trying to distract him, but he didn't turn around. I saw something fly off the top of the arroyo directly above him. It was Marie. She hit him in the back with her knees like a human cannonball. He fell forward and there was a loud crack, but it didn't come from the rifle.

When I reached them, Marie was standing over Earl trying to catch her breath. Earl was facedown, not moving, and for a second I thought he was dead, but he rolled over and let out an agonized yell.

"My leg!"

His left cowboy boot was twisted at an impossible angle, and his left arm didn't look much better. The crack I heard must have been his leg breaking over the snag when Marie hit him.

"Are you okay?" I asked Marie.

"I'm fine."

"Where did you come from?"

"Buckley dropped Dad and me off near the arroyo, then hid the camper someplace. We saw Earl running, and I took off after him."

Uncle John arrived at the top of the arroyo and made his way to the bottom.

He looked down at Earl. "Did you shoot Hank?" he asked, calmly.

"No!" Earl said through clenched teeth.

"You're lying." Uncle John reached into his pocket and pulled out the shell casings he had picked up earlier and showed them to him. "Your boot prints are all over the place." He walked over and picked up Earl's rifle. He ejected a shell from it and compared it to the casings in his hand. They were the same caliber and brand. "Where's your truck, Earl?" he asked.

Earl told him, and Uncle John reached down and pulled the keys out of his pocket. Buckley drove up to the edge of the arroyo with the camper. Uncle John gave the keys to Marie. "Buckley will take you to his truck. Drive it over here. Jake and I are going to need it."

Marie stared at her father without saying anything.

"I know you have no reason to help this boy," he said. "But we need to get him to the hospital. I want you and Buckley to drive him there in the camper."

"What are you going to use his truck for?"

"To bring the lobo in."

"Can you drive?" she asked him.

"I think so," he replied.

Marie climbed the bank.

"Did you get the dart off?" Uncle John asked.

"Yeah, and I think I hit it."

"If that's the case, the lobo will be lying somewhere up the arroyo. If you didn't, it will be long gone. Before we look we need to help them get Earl up the bank. And we'll need to splint his leg."

I started looking for a branch that would work. We splinted Earl's leg and dragged him up the bank, which wasn't too comfortable for him, if his yowling was any indication. Uncle John had picked up the crates I had stashed and put them in the camper. We pulled them out along with a noose pole and laid Earl on one of the beds in the camper.

"We'll see you back at the house," Uncle John said. Marie and Buckley got into the camper and drove away.

Uncle John pushed both crates over the edge.

"Why do we need two crates?" I asked.

"Let's go find the lobo," he said.

We found the wolf about a hundred yards up the arroyo lying under an old log with its eyes wide open and its tongue lolling out over its yellowed teeth. The tranquilizer had done its job.

John took a close look at the teeth. "An old lobo," he said. "Seven or eight years, I'd guess." He pulled the dart out. "Run back and get a crate. This lobo needs to go home."

I brought a crate down and we put the lobo inside it. After we got the lobo loaded onto the bed of Earl's truck, I told Uncle John that I'd get the second crate and bring it up.

"We're not quite finished," he said. He gave me the noose pole and a shovel, then slid back down the bank to the bottom of the arroyo.

I followed him down. "What's going on?"

"Grab the crate and follow me."

"Is there another lobo?"

"We'll see."

I followed him up the arroyo. When we got to the hollow, I stopped and pulled my water bottle from its hiding place and drank about half of it before taking it away from my lips.

Uncle John smiled. "Bottle fell down, huh?"

"Yeah."

He led me about two hundred yards farther up the arroyo and stopped. "See that hole up there?" He pointed to a crack in the bank about five feet above our heads with a narrow ledge in front of it. "Crawl up there and widen it. Don't be surprised by what you find."

I climbed up and widened the hole, thinking a second lobo would jump out at me any moment. When I had the opening big enough to get my shoulders through, Uncle John tossed a small flashlight up to me. I shined it into the opening. It was a cavern about six feet deep and three feet high. In the corner were four sets of yellow eyes.

"How many are there?" John called out from behind me.

I backed my shoulders out of the cavern and turned around. "Four. You knew all the time?"

"Nope," he said. "But I had a hunch." He picked the crate up with both hands and passed it up to me. His left arm seemed to be working fine. He climbed up and joined me. I pulled the pups out one at a time with the noose pole. Before we put them in the crate, Uncle John checked each one.

"Male . . . female . . . female . . . male . . . By the size of their large ears, little heads, and gangly legs, I'd say they're about two months old."

Marie and Buckley were waiting for us when we got back to the ranch. She helped me move the crates into the wolf shed and transfer two of the pups into another crate so they would have more room. Taw, Betty, Buckley, and Uncle John watched us.

"Okay," Uncle John said. "Now let's discuss what we're going to do with our little pack of lobos."

"I thought we'd already decided," I said.

"That was before we had five of them."

"Earl was telling everyone at the hospital that he shot the lobo," Marie said with disgust.

"And what did you say?" Uncle John asked.

"Nothing."

"Good!" Uncle John was delighted. "We'll just let Earl think he shot the lobo. In fact, I'll put the word out that I followed the blood trail, but couldn't find the body. I'll tell everyone that judging by the amount of blood, there is no way the lobo could have survived. This will make the job of getting the three lobos into Mexico much easier."

"Three?"

Uncle John nodded. "While you and I are taking the lobos across the border, Marie and Buckley can drive a male and female over to Rand's."

I stared at him. "But I thought . . ."

"The lobo is pretty old. I suspect she and her mate left Mexico long before she whelped, and somewhere along the way he got killed. Raising these four pups on her own has just about taken everything out of her. She'll have a lot easier time raising two pups down in Mexico rather than four."

"What will I tell Rand?" Marie asked.

"Tell him that I found them along the side of a road in a cardboard box and that I think they're Mexican wolves."

*   *   *

Uncle John was eager to get his plan started before people discovered we had the lobos. He and Marie drove to Polacca to spread the rumor about the dead lobo and to call his Mexican friend, Flaco.

While they were gone I asked Taw if he wanted to go with us.

"I don't think so," he said. "I made a promise to myself when I got to Hopiland."

"What's that?"

"I promised myself that I would never leave here again. I have work to do here. You and John take the lobos home."

s e v e n t e e n

Uncle John and I left early the next morning for Mexico. It was a Friday. He wanted to cross the border that night because it would be easier to get the lobos across during the heavy weekend traffic. We drove all day and into the evening, keeping each other awake by talking. Uncle John told me some amazing stories about wolves.

When we got to the border, Uncle John spoke to the guards in what sounded like perfect Spanish. I don't know what he said, but they started laughing and waved us through without even looking in the back of the camper.

By the time we got to Flaco's house high in the mountains, the sun was up. Uncle John and I were exhausted. Flaco came running out, and he and Uncle John hugged each other. Flaco was about Uncle John's age, with white hair combed straight back. He introduced us to his son, daughter-in-law, and three grandchildren who lived with him. He told us we would release the lobos the next morning.

"It will take us all night to drive to the place," he said in English. "But there is time now for you to eat and rest."

Late Saturday evening we loaded the lobos into Flaco's four-wheel drive truck and headed farther up into the mountains in back of his home. It was rugged country with steep hills, pine-covered ridges, and small streams running down the valleys. It looked like a good place for the lobo and her pups to live.

Flaco told us he knew the female lobo. He recognized her by Uncle John's description of her prints. He had seen these prints often, but he had caught a glimpse of her only once when she was much younger. It had been more than a year since he had seen her tracks, and he had thought she was dead.

I asked him if they were still trapping lobos in Mexico.

He laughed and shook his head. "There are no more lobos in Mexico. Trappers are not interested in catching ghosts."

We drove all night up and down the hills, along ridges, and over trails that looked as though they hadn't been driven on for years.

At dawn we arrived at a small clearing. Flaco stopped the truck. "This is the lobo's old home," he said. "The home of the ghosts."

We took the crates out of the back and set them in the middle of the clearing.

"The little ones first," he said. "This way they will see their mother leave her crate and follow her."

I looked at Uncle John. "You caught them," he said. "You have to let them go."

I opened the crate door, but the pups didn't budge. "What do I do now?"

Flaco pointed to their mother's crate. "Move it back to the edge of the clearing behind the other crate." I pulled it back. "Now open the door. She will go."

I opened the door and stepped behind the crate. The female stumbled out, took a few unsteady steps, then stopped. She turned her head and stared at me for a second or two as if she didn't know she was free.

"You're home," I said.

She ran across the clearing, hesitating for a moment as she passed the second crate. When the pups saw her, they bounded out. The lobo looked back one more time, but it wasn't to see me. She was making sure her pups were following her.

When we arrived back at Uncle John's two days later, it looked like an entire construction crew was working on the house.

Doc jumped down from the roof and ran over to the camper. He threw his arm's around me, then held me out at arm's length. "I understand that you've been breaking federal endangered species laws."

"I have no idea what you're talking about," I said innocently.

"That is the perfect answer," he said.

"When did you get here?"

"I drove over with Rand and Sandra yesterday."

Uncle John came around the other side of the camper. He and Doc shook hands.

Uncle John stared at his house. A lot of work had been done since we left. Taw and the others came over. Nicole was carrying Hannah. I was pleased to see both of them.

"What have you done to my home?" Uncle John asked in mock anger.

Taw grinned. "I'm just getting started."

Uncle John looked at Marie. "What about Earl?"

"His next stop after the hospital is prison," she said. "Using the rifle was a parole violation. And this time they say he's going to serve his entire term."

"And you're going sailing across the ocean, Cousin Jake," Hannah said.

I looked at Nicole. "I am?"

"Well, we'd like you to," Nicole said.

I looked at Doc to see what he thought of this plan. "It's okay with me," he said. "As long as you come back to the jaguar preserve in the fall. I need your help."

"I don't even know how to sail."

Rand stepped forward. "Nicole has generously offered to teach you," he said. Nicole turned bright red, and I'm sure my face was about the same shade.

"How are the wolf pups?" I asked, trying to change the subject.

"The preliminary DNA on them looks pretty good," Rand said. "Indications are they're the real thing."

"They are," I said.

Rand held his hand up. "I don't want to hear another word. I've had a hard enough time explaining where they came from. They were a little suspicious of the cardboard box explanation."

Uncle John held the camper keys out to Buckley. "I believe these are yours."

"Maybe not," Buckley said. "I know we had a deal, but I won't be needing the camper anymore."

"Why not?"

"I've got a job." He looked at Doc.

"It's a shame to let a good biologist go to waste," Doc said. "And since Jake's going sailing, we'll need someone to take his place. Buckley's going back to Brazil with me."

"You better go inside and get some rest," Betty said to Uncle John.

"I feel just fine."

"Well, Tawupu has an outing planned," she said. "He's just been waiting for you to come back."

"What now?" Uncle John asked.

"You'll see," Taw said. "I don't know if you're up to it or not."

"I'm up to anything you can devise, old root."

At dawn the following morning we were walking up the steep trail to Taw's mesa. Uncle John led the way. We reached the top just as the sun rose above the horizon.

"It's been a long time," Taw said.

"Too long, friend," Uncle John said.

We stood on the edge in a row and watched the desert below turn different colors.

"Uncle Buckley gave me a kachina doll," Hannah said. "He says it's a wolf kachina."

I looked at the carving. It was pretty good.

"Why do wolves howl?" Hannah asked.

"I don't know, but we have several experts here."

"It's one of the ways they talk to one another," Rand said.

"You know what I think," Taw said. "I think they do because it makes them feel good. They do it for the *howl* of it."

Uncle John cupped both hands around his mouth and began. We all joined in. When we finished we listened for a reply. The only answer we heard was the wind.

ACKNOWLEDGMENTS

I would like to thank the following people for their valuable time and comments: Melanie Gill, Barbara Kouts, Mike Phillips, Michael Roydon, Zach Teters, Pat Washington, and of course my wonderful wife and best friend, Marie. You did a *howl* of a good job!

Roland enjoys hearing from his readers. You can contact him by accessing his Web page at: **www.rolandsmith.com** or writing him at P.O. Box 911, Tualatin, OR 97062.